Agreeing to do his fellow vampire enforcer a favor, Nereo Belmonte heads to Stone Ridge, Colorado. He thought the task sounded simple enough — search the minds of four men who'd been experimented on and see if he can restore their memories. To his surprise, when Nereo walks into the room, he finds himself drawn to the blood of one of them — Warren Berger. With a vested interest in the job, Nereo worries the mental fog he encounters may never clear, leaving Warren's mind in danger of returning to the experiments' original programming.

Warren knows his name. He knows his duty — follow Doctor Winoan's orders. Everything else is immaterial. Except, when Winoan orders him to kill a man, he hears a noise that makes him question that — a snarling hiss that sounds like an order to stop. To Warren's surprise, something deep within his psyche responds, and he obeys, as does his three team members. The odd presence in his mind decides that the speaker — a cheetah, which turns into a man — is their new leader. Warren doesn't understand what's going on, but he has no choice but to obey.

Upon meeting Nereo, that voice in Warren's head purrs with delight. Warren agrees — he wants the man. While peering into Nereo's red-irised gaze, odd images flood his mind, clouding him with confusion and distrust. Can Warren learn to trust Nereo, allowing him to help, before those who worked with his old boss finds a way to counter his internal voice's control and steal him back?

Connecting with an Altered
Copyright © 2021 Charlie Richards
ISBN: 978-1-4874-3405-2
Cover art by Angela Waters

Published by eXtasy Books Inc

Look for us online at:
www.eXtasybooks.com

Connecting with an Altered
Wolves of Stone Ridge 56

By

Charlie Richards

DEDICATION

Man cannot discover new oceans unless he has the courage to lose sight of the shore.
~Andre Gide

CHAPTER ONE

"I really appreciate you doing this for us."

Nereo Belmonte relaxed in his office chair and stared at the ceiling as he replied to fellow vampire enforcer, Vince Marché. "You're welcome, Vince." Grinning, he added, "Besides, the rumor-mill is all about how the Stone Ridge pack has been blessed by Fate, what with all the mate-matches those guys have found . . . you included."

Less than a decade before, Nereo never would have believed that Vince would end up with a shifter beloved. The other Vampire Council enforcer had avoided shifters at all costs. He'd been more than a little prejudiced against them, too—a result of his upbringing.

Times do change.

"That's true," Vince replied, and Nereo could hear the happiness in the other vampire's voice.

And he has every right to be.

"Maybe you'll find your beloved there," Vince continued.

"From your lips to Fate's ears," Nereo quipped back, a smile curving his lips. At almost two hundred years of age, Nereo had been waiting a long time to find his soul mate. He couldn't give a rat's ass who it turned out to be. "I'll fly out in the morning."

"Good luck, my friend."

"Thanks, Vince," Nereo replied before lowering his phone from his ear. A press of his thumb disconnected the call, and he tossed the device onto the desk. Lifting his arms over his head, Nereo stretched, arching his back and flexing his arms.

1

The twinge to his right side reminded him that he was still healing.

"Another day, and I'll be right as rain," Nereo muttered as he lowered his arms. With a sigh, he rose to his feet and headed out of his home office. "Can't believe that bastard managed to get the drop on me."

Still, Nereo had taken down the rogue vampire. He'd walked away with deep claw wounds raked along the right side of his rib cage, but he *had* walked away. The rogue hadn't.

Nereo strode into his bedroom and pulled out a large duffel bag. As he began packing, he thought about Vince's request.

Vince and his three buddies were already on assignment, so they couldn't help out their friends in Stone Ridge. The alpha there — Alpha Declan McIntire — had requested their aid in peering into the minds of four soldiers who'd been experimented on. Evidently, they didn't respond to any commands other than who they perceived as their alpha.

As part of their experimentation, the men had been programmed to think their alpha was the scientist doing the experiments — Doctor Winoan. Then the doctor had begun using them as his personal bodyguards. Evidently, he'd realized his life was in danger.

That hadn't stopped the wolf pack from capturing the doctor, though. Of course, it was by dumb luck that they'd stumbled upon the group's real leader — Bailey Dyer. The man had been their unit commander, and he'd been smuggled out of the scientist's facility by his brother — Ronan. Ronan had ended up mating with a wolf shifter, and they'd helped alter the experiments done on Bailey, saving the man's memories.

As Nereo folded a couple of pairs of polo shirts and placed them in the bag on top of his jeans, he marveled at Fate's unique design.

Hope I'm going to be in there somewhere soon. Maybe I'll ask to meet all the single wolf shifters.

Nereo wouldn't mind a shifter beloved.

I wouldn't mind a human beloved, either.

Whoever Fate ended up sending him, Nereo knew the other half of his soul would be just perfect.

Smiling, Nereo chuckled under his breath at his thoughts. He felt a fissure of anticipation slither up his spine. Hope, he decided.

After finishing his packing, Nereo headed to his kitchen. He opened the fridge and pulled out a bottle full of red liquid. After popping the cap, he brought it to his lips and took a gulp.

Nereo grimaced at the taste of the cold blood. While he always had the stuff on hand, it would never be a favorite. Still, he knew he needed the sustenance before heading to the wolf shifter pack the next day. With his healing injury, Nereo needed more than his standard once-a-week donor, and he didn't feel like hunting right then.

With the bottle still half-full, Nereo grabbed the tomato juice. He poured it into the blood and put the juice away before screwing the cap back on it. Then he tipped the bottle back and forth, mixing the two liquids.

Once Nereo reopened the bottle, he took another swig. Grunting with pleasure, he headed toward his living room, ready to make his version of a bloody mary. Turning on the TV, he found a show to watch. Then Nereo poured himself a whiskey from the sideboard, adding a couple of shots to the bottle, too. Taking both drinks, he settled in his favorite recliner and relaxed for the night.

"What kind of vehicle do you want us to have available to you when you arrive?"

Nereo had just finished making his way through security when the call from Beta Dixon Holsteen came through his line. Slinging the strap of his bag over his shoulder, he thought swiftly. He tried to decide what would be a fun vehicle to wander around the mountain roads of Colorado.

With a grin, Nereo couldn't help but ask, "You wouldn't happen to have a motorcycle I could borrow, would you?"

Beta Dixon's deep chuckle sounded through the line. "You're one of those, huh?"

"I own a *Harley*," Nereo stated, surprised by the beta's teasing, but he was happy to roll with it. Vince had told him that the pack was fairly laid-back, so hearing the confirmation pleased him. "But driving across country would take a couple of days, and I figured you needed me there before that."

In truth, driving cross-country hadn't even crossed his mind when Vince had approached him with his request.

"Well, I think I can arrange that for you, Nereo," Beta Dixon told him, his voice full of warmth. "With you flying out here, you'll probably need all the gear, too, right?"

"I will," Nereo confirmed, his anticipation ramping up. "Maybe after I see to these guys you need help with, I'll take a few days to explore." Realizing how bold that statement was—inviting himself to wander around a wolf pack's territory—Nereo quickly amended, "If that's okay with your al—um, you all."

Damn. No talking about alpha's in the middle of a human airport.

As much as Nereo would have loved to have taken one of the Vampire Council's jets, none had been available. Instead, he was taking a commercial flight. At least he didn't have to pay for it, and he was flying first class.

"I'm sure that won't be an issue, Enforcer Nereo," Beta Dixon replied. "When does your flight land?"

"Twelve-seventeen," Nereo replied, catching sight of a sign that indicated the gate he needed. He turned in that direction and strode swiftly down the corridor. "Thank you again for the transportation."

Chuckling gruffly, Beta Dixon reminded, "You're doing us

a favor, so no worries." Before Nereo could reply, the beta added, "Your contact is Kade McGraw, one of our enforcers. I'll text you his number."

"Thank you again," Nereo replied dutifully. "I've never been to the mountains of Colorado. I'm looking forward to it."

"See you soon," Beta Dixon replied before disconnecting the call.

Nereo located his gate, found a seat, and pulled up a reading app on his phone, settling in to wait for his flight to board.

Twenty minutes later, Nereo heard the announcement for handicapped boarding on his flight. He pulled up his electronic ticket on his phone and rose to his feet, knowing first class would be called shortly. When it was, Nereo approached the gate with several others.

Standing in line, Nereo couldn't help the way his gaze fixated on the slacks-covered butt of the human man in front of him. The fabric pulled enticingly with each step the male made, showcasing firm, round cheeks. Sliding his attention higher, he took in the slender, muscular arm pulling the rolling suitcase behind him.

Hmm . . . a businessman who keeps himself in shape. Too bad his cologne is hiding his natural scent, although it's fairly nice.

The man's short business cut showed off a strong neck, and Nereo licked his fangs as his keen vampire sight spotted the perfect place to feed from.

I wonder if he'd be interested in joining the mile-high club.

As the thought flickered through Nereo's mind, the man strode away from him, moving down the tunnel to get on the plane. He held up his phone to be scanned, still staring at the male.

"Is something wrong, sir?" the woman at the gate asked, glancing over her shoulder at the retreating human.

Nereo yanked his focus away from the guy to offer her a

reassuring smile. "No, everything is fine," he told her. "Just eager to get where I'm going."

She smiled and nodded. "Have a nice flight."

"Thank you."

Heading down the tunnel, Nereo turned a corner and spotted the plane's open door. Another attendant waited, and he followed his instructions to locate his seat. A quick glance around showed Nereo the nicely dressed male easing into a seat two rows up. After sitting in his own seat, he leaned down and stowed his bag beneath the chair in front of him. When Nereo straightened, he watched the guy lean toward the woman beside him, and they pecked briefly.

Oh well. Not like I need the sustenance.

Dismissing the hottie, Nereo changed his phone to airplane mode and returned to his book.

The flight was uneventful and landed on time, for which Nereo was grateful. Once they'd docked with the airport terminal, he grabbed his bag and followed the others off the plane. With the strap slung over his shoulder, Nereo made his way through the airport, following the exit signs.

Nereo slowed his steps, peering around the area near the doors. Spotting a large, dark-haired man holding a sign with his first name on it, he headed that way. Before he'd taken three steps, the guy riveted a dark-eyed gaze on him. When the male arched one thick eyebrow in silent question while glancing at the sign he held, Nereo dipped his head in acknowledgment.

As Nereo approached, the man folded his sign in half while turning and speaking to someone. A much shorter and slenderer man pushed away from the wall he'd been leaning against. The other guy reached the bigger man first and took the sign from him. The first male slung his now-free arm around the smaller man's waist before focusing on Nereo again.

"I'm Kade," the man greeted, holding out one large hand. "Nereo, right?"

Taking Kade's palm in his own, Nereo shook and released. "I am," he confirmed again. "Nice to meet you. Thanks for meeting me."

Kade nodded. "No problem." He tipped his chin and indicated the other man. "This is my mate, Tom."

Nereo shook the other man's hand. Even over the smells of the airport, he could still catch Tom's human scent drenched in wolf shifter. "Nice to meet you, too."

"And you," Tom replied before pressing back into Kade's hold.

"Do you have any luggage to grab?" Kade asked, pointing toward the pick-up area.

Shaking his head, Nereo lifted the shoulder that the strap rested on. "I like to travel light."

Kade's goateed lips curved into a small smile. "I don't blame you. Let's head out, then."

"With pleasure."

Turning, Kade and Tom led the way out of the airport. They crossed a couple of streets where cars were dropping people off or picking them up. Busses crept by as well as taxis.

Once they entered a parking garage, Kade turned his head and focused on him. "Heard from Dixon that you wanted a motorcycle."

Nereo nodded. "Best way to travel, in my opinion."

"Man after my own heart," Kade replied.

In Nereo's opinion, Tom's growl sounded so damn cute. "Better not be after your heart," he grumbled. "That's mine."

Kade laughed as he dipped his head and pecked a kiss to the side of Tom's head. "Yeah, it is, baby."

Chuckling softly, Nereo assured, "Have no fear, Tom. I would never disrespect a mate-bond in such a way."

"Sorry," Tom muttered, a slight flush rising in his cheeks.

"Sometimes, these territorial urges take me by surprise."

Nereo nodded. "No worries." Although he'd never experienced them himself, he'd heard from others that they could be intense.

"Here we are." Kade indicated a pair of motorcycles situated in one space. "Here." He tossed a set of keys to Nereo, which he deftly caught. "That's to the *Harley*."

Grinning with pleasure—and a little surprise, considering the expense of the machine—Nereo hummed. "Gorgeous. Thank you." The other bike was a very nice *Goldwing*, and it would have been a fantastic ride, too, but Nereo couldn't help but be pleased by the wolf pack's generosity. "Your people are too kind."

"Don't put a scratch on my baby," Kade growled in warning as he opened one of the *Goldwing's* saddlebags. "Or I'll take it outa your hide."

Snapping his attention away from the high-end machine, Nereo focused on Kade. While the man smiled, the gleam in his dark-brown eyes told him he was deadly serious. It hit him that Kade was loaning him one of his own, personal bikes.

Nereo dipped his head in acknowledgment. "I'll treat it with the utmost care."

Kade nodded before pulling a leather jacket out of the saddlebag and holding it out. "Try this on."

Five minutes later, geared up with a leather jacket and chaps as well as a helmet, Nereo used an offered bungee to strap his duffel bag to the back of the bike.

Then they were on their way.

As Nereo followed Kade—with Tom riding behind him— city streets soon gave way to country roads. He peered left and right, enjoying the scenery. Climbing higher, pines of several varieties closed in around them, and Nereo breathed deeply of the fresh, clean air.

Magnificent.

The nip in the fall air revealed why Kade had insisted on the chaps. The leaves on the occasional deciduous trees they passed were full of vibrant orange and red leaves. When they slowed and passed through Stone Ridge, Kade pointed out the necessities — grocery store, best place for fuel, great local restaurants, and a fantastic bed and breakfast.

After another fifteen minutes on narrow winding roads, Kade turned onto a gravel driveway.

Nereo followed, taking care on the loose rock. The trees parted a few seconds later, and he found himself staring at a large, lodge-style home. The bottom half of the structure was covered in stonework, giving way to gorgeous dark wood up top.

Impressed, Nereo just sat and stared for a few seconds after parking and shutting off his bike. "Beautiful," he murmured softly. "How many of the pack live here?"

Nereo knew that Declan's pack boasted nearly a hundred members, at least half of them mated, and not all of them were wolf shifters. If he had to guess, he thought the place could hold a good fifteen or more comfortably.

"Right now . . ." Kade hummed and squinted, obviously thinking. "Ten. Alpha Declan and Lark. Myself and Tom. Then the four altered humans, their altered leader — Bailey, and Bailey's mate, Clayton."

While Nereo found it interesting that more enforcers or even the beta didn't live with the alpha, he simply nodded.

To each his own.

"Come on," Kade encouraged. "I'm ready for a cup of coffee. How about you?"

Getting off the bike, Nereo smiled. "I wouldn't say no."

CHAPTER TWO

Warren Berger sat in the large bedroom where he'd been ordered by his leader—a man he'd learned was Bailey Dyer. Bailey hadn't been Warren's original leader. No, that had been Doctor Winoan.

When Warren had woken from what the doctor said was a coma due to being exposed to an experimental nerve gas, he hadn't remembered anything. The only thing he knew was that Doctor Winoan's word was law. The other three men, who he'd been told were part of his team, had all seemed to agree, following the man's orders, too.

All that had changed just a few weeks before.

It had been a normal day where Warren and the others acted as bodyguards to Doctor Winoan when he'd needed to take a meeting at a research facility. It had all been pretty standard until an alarm had gone off. Warren's first instinct had been to evacuate Doctor Winoan.

Instead, Doctor Winoan had ordered another man—Doctor Nerian—to escort them all to see Doctor Kuzmich's project. The project had turned out to be a cheetah in a cage. Kuzmich had shot something into the cheetah, waking it from sleep . . . then he'd hit Winoan with a tranquilizer dart.

As Winoan had sank to the floor, he'd ordered Warren and his team to kill Kuzmich. When he'd moved to respond, the cheetah had snarled ferally. For some reason, the sound reverberated through Warren, waking something within him—something with a *presence*.

Warren had stopped, confused. His team members had

done the same, clearly in the same boat. The noise came again, and Warren thought it sounded distinctly like an order to stand down, to back off . . . just without words.

For some reason, that newly woken presence within Warren responded, and he found he couldn't take another step. As much as he tried to obey a now-unconscious Winoan's order, he couldn't. The presence in his mind somehow took control of his body, forcing him to accept a new leader — the cat in the cage.

Doctor Kuzmich had then forced Nerian to unlock the cage before tranquilizing him, too.

With his head bowed in submission, unable to do much more than shuffle his feet, Warren had watched as Kuzmich had released the cheetah. The cheetah had rubbed his head against the man as if he were a housecat, and Kuzmich responded by rubbing its ears and whispering words of endearment. Warren hadn't understood . . . until the cheetah changed into a man.

For some reason, seeing the dark-haired male, Warren felt a niggle of recognition, as if he should know who the male was. Except, that was ridiculous. He would surely recall where and when he had met a man who could transform into a cheetah.

Didn't such things only exist in fairy tales?

Guess not, because one's standing right in front of me.

To Warren's surprise, after donning Doctor Nerian's lab coat to hide his nakedness, the cat-turned-man had spoken to them . . . by name. He'd known each and every one of them. Warren just didn't know how that was possible.

And now, here I sit in the bedroom of a lodge in the woods . . . somewhere.

The presence in Warren's mind was happy to do whatever Bailey ordered. That included allowing a small blond man introduced as Doctor Lark Trystan to take his blood pressure and draw blood. He'd been assigned to this room on the second floor, given t-shirts and sweats, and been ordered to the bathroom to clean up and change.

They brought him food several times a day and asked him questions about what he remembered. Warren had shared what he knew, which wasn't much. After waking from the gas-induced coma, he'd teamed up with the others under Winoan's command.

Bailey had appeared extremely distressed that none of them remembered him. That had been the hardest part. The presence in his mind didn't like it when Bailey was upset. Warren had felt the urge to do whatever was necessary to soothe the male. Except, he could do nothing other than follow the guy's orders, and he hoped that would be enough.

The rev of motorcycle engines caught his attention. Someone had arrived. He wished his room faced the front of the house, so he could look to see if he recognized whoever it was, but his windows faced the back, giving him an endless view of pines.

Before long, Warren heard the front door open and the rumble of masculine voices. His sensitive hearing allowed him to make out some of what was said, and he realized Alpha Declan was being introduced to someone—Nereo, he thought. The guy was welcomed and offered coffee, which was accepted.

They must have moved to a different area of the house after that because their voices faded.

With a sigh, Warren rubbed the back of his neck. He rose and crossed to the window. Leaning against the frame, he crossed his arms over his shirt-covered chest and crossed one bare ankle over the other.

As Warren had been doing for the last couple of weeks, he could do nothing but wait. While he'd been given permission to use the facilities whenever he felt the need, he hadn't been given leave to roam the house. Every morning when he woke, he went through his morning exercise regime in his bedroom before cleaning up for the day. From the noises in the other rooms, Warren knew his team members were doing the same. They bypassed each other in the halls, grunting a greeting, but beyond that, there wasn't anything for them to talk about.

Warren stared at the trees and waited . . . and waited. He could have turned on the TV in the room, but he didn't care to watch anything. While he wasn't certain why, he knew that had never been a way he enjoyed passing the time.

Glancing toward the books sitting on the nightstand, Warren considered reading one. Declan had shown him to the small library on the first floor, allowing him to take whatever he'd wished. Warren had read three of the five books already and was halfway through the fourth.

As much as Warren enjoyed them, that odd presence within him was unsettled, affecting him, too. He wished he could figure out what the hell it was. Bailey and the others referred to it as his other half—his shifter half—but that couldn't be right.

Because I'm not a shifter.

Warren heard footsteps on the stairs, pulling him out of his thoughts. Cocking his head, he tried to discern how many people approached.

Three . . . and I recognize the tread of two of them.

Once more, Declan and Bailey were going to visit with at least one of them. He wasn't certain about the cadence of the last person. An educated guess would make it the stranger— Nereo.

For some reason, the prospect of meeting him caused anticipation to zip through his veins.

Weird.

A light knock sounded at his door, followed by Bailey asking, "Warren, may we come in?"

"Of course," Warren replied, turning and straightening. As

soon as the door opened and Bailey appeared, he dipped his head in submission. "How may I be of assistance, sir?"

Bailey blew out a quiet breath as something flickered across his expression. It was there and gone so swiftly that Warren wasn't certain what it meant. Then Bailey moved to the side, and he was joined by Declan and a stranger—a black-haired man with smoldering good looks and a broad, strong body that Warren suddenly had the desire to rub up against, as if *he* were the cheetah shifter.

"Oh," the man murmured in a deep rumbling voice. His deep brown eyes narrowed as he tipped his head to the side just a little. He met Warren's gaze and held it, staring at him intensely. Ever-so-softly, he whispered, "This is . . . unexpected."

"What's unexpected?" Declan asked, half-turned to face everyone. He must have seen something in the stranger's expression, for he asked, "Nereo, what's wrong?"

Nereo snapped his focus to Declan, and Warren wanted to growl, to demand it back on him. Maintaining control, he resisted . . . barely.

"I believe this man is my beloved," Nereo told Declan.

While Warren didn't know what that meant, Declan obviously did. His black brows shot up, lifting high on his forehead. He glanced from Warren to Nereo and back a couple of times.

"Are ye certain?" Declan asked, his light Irish accent deepening, betraying his surprise.

Nereo tipped his head in a small nod as he refocused back on Warren, making his inner self damn near purr. "As much as a vampire can be without tasting his blood."

Vampire? What the hell?

"Do ye wish to ask his permission to taste him?" Declan asked, as if that made any sense at all.

Nereo nodded slowly. "I suppose I better." He glanced at Bailey. "A vampire is drawn to their beloved by the scent of their blood, but tasting it confirms that the person is the other half of their soul." Arching a dark brow, Nereo took several slow steps toward Warren. "Will you answer my questions? Or must they come from your alpha?"

Warren opened his mouth, then hesitated. Even as he wanted to answer so badly, his conditioning made it difficult. After a glance toward Bailey, Warren focused on Nereo again. "I—" he began before stopping.

"Warren, you are welcome to answer any question Nereo poses," Bailey told him. Then he added, "And this is Nereo Belmonte. He's here to try to help."

Nodding once, Warren replied, "Yes, sir." He glanced his leader's way once more before returning his focus to Nereo. He couldn't seem to tear his gaze away from him for long.

Nereo was, in a word, glorious. His shoulders were broad under his polo shirt. His arms sported thick muscles, and the comfortable-looking jeans encasing his legs molded to him like a second skin. Nereo stood a couple of inches over Warren's six-foot-two, and with the way the man peered down at him, his shaggy black hair fell across his forehead in thick waves that Warren wanted to tuck behind his ears.

Still, Warren couldn't help but ask, "What's a vampire, sir?"

While Warren understood the word, in theory, that couldn't be true. After all, there were no such things as blood-sucking creatures of the night. Not to mention, the sun was high in the afternoon sky, streaming in through the window.

The corners of Nereo's lips twitched as he answered for Bailey. "A vampire is a paranormal being, just as a shifter is. We just have different traits." With a wink and a grin, which showed off far-too-pointed canines, Nereo added, "Whatever ridiculous stories you've heard about vampires, other than the blood-drinking thing, they're most likely not true."

"Blood-drinking," Warren repeated slowly, narrowing his

eyes. "You drink blood?"

The sharp teeth would make sense. I mean, before a couple of weeks ago, I didn't believe shifters were real. Why not vampires, too?

Nereo nodded once, a smirk curving up the left side of his lips. "Indeed." With a wink and another step closer, he claimed, "But sunlight doesn't bother us, we also need regular food to survive, and I happen to love garlic."

Then Nereo stood less than six inches before Warren, and the man's citrusy scent filled his nostrils . . . and his mouth watered. Warren stared at Nereo's full lips, wanting a taste so damn badly.

Damn. When was the last time I kissed a man?

While his three team members had all fidgeted with discomfort upon seeing the gay couples' affections toward each other, Warren hadn't. Somewhere in his psyche, he accepted that he enjoyed kissing men, too. Something told him that this man's kiss would surpass any other . . . if he could remember them.

"I do enjoy the way you're looking at me, Warren," Nereo rumbled. Lifting both hands, he hesitated before asking, "May I touch you? I wish to kiss you."

Warren was more than on board with that. His blood roared through his veins, the odd presence in his mind offered a rumbly purr, expressing his own excitement, and his dick quickly filled. He wanted Nereo's mouth against his own . . . and so much more.

"Yes," Warren replied simply.

"Thank you."

To Warren's pleasure, Nereo didn't say more. He rested one hand on Warren's hip and the other on his jaw. Dipping his head the couple of inches needed, Nereo sealed his mouth over Warren's.

The first press of Nereo's lips to his own caused tingles to dance down his neck, wringing a gasp of surprise from him. A light swipe of Nereo's tongue along his bottom lip was all the warning he received before the other man slid the append-age between his parted lips. The delicious taste of man and citrus burst across Warren's taste buds, drawing a moan from deep within him.

Unable to help himself, Warren gripped Nereo's upper arms, needing the contact. As the other man used the hold on his jaw to tip his head just a smidge, he deepened the kiss. Warren welcomed the better contact, enjoying the glide of his tongue along his own as the man explored his mouth in smooth, masterful sweeps.

Warren eased his tongue into Nereo's mouth to do a little exploring of his own. The prick of pain when Nereo pushed Warren's tongue along his sharp teeth was instantly soothed when he suckled his tongue, causing fiery tingles to rush through his bloodstream.

The presence in Warren's mind rumbled with delight, and he had to agree. His cock throbbed in his sweatpants, and he felt an almost irresistible urge to step close, to flush their bodies. He wanted to rock his hips, to rut against the bigger man.

Nereo eased the kiss to an end. His grip on Warren's hip tightened, holding him in place as if he'd been able to read his mind. Resting his forehead against Warren's own, Nereo panted along with Warren, their breaths mingling.

"You are definitely mine, Warren," Nereo stated, his voice deep and husky with obvious lust. "May I try to help you?"

It took two hard swallows for Warren to get his voice to work. "H-How do you p-plan to do that?"

Sliding his hand to cup Warren's nape, Nereo told him, "A vampire has the ability to peer into another person's mind. I wish to see if I can draw your memories forward to help you recollect them."

Warren hesitated a few seconds before nodding once. He didn't know if he believed that the man was actually a vampire or if he could truly do as he said, but he figured it was worth a shot. If the man was actually crazy, what did it hurt to try?

"Thank you, my beloved," Nereo rumbled. "Just look into my eyes and relax your mind."

While Warren had no idea how to relax his mind, he could at least do the first part. It was certainly no hardship to stare into Nereo's intense, dark-brown eyes.

Suddenly, the brown bled away to be dominated by dark-red irises, and the man's pupils contracted, nearly disappearing.

Warren felt something cool creep over his mind. At first, he thought it was that presence he'd been experiencing for the past couple of weeks. Except, *that* presence seemed to be welcoming this new sensation.

Just as quickly as his confusion surfaced, images began to flash through him. They were murky, difficult to make out, but the pain they brought racked his body. Agony flooded him, replacing the fiery bliss of just seconds before.

Jerking in Nereo's hold, Warren tried to twist away, but the other man held him fast.

Unable to help himself, Warren screamed.

CHAPTER THREE

The sound of his beloved's agony bouncing off the walls tore at Nereo's heart. He severed the connection, drawing out of his man's mind as swiftly as he could. Still, by the time he'd ended the trance, Warren slumped in his arms.

"Fuck," Nereo cried, swinging his unconscious Warren into his arms. Cradling him to his chest, he turned and faced Declan and Bailey. "I saw —"

The thud of bare feet pounded in the corridor. A second later, three men streamed into the room. An expression of barely leashed aggression was etched on each of their features.

Spotting Warren in Nereo's arms, they spread out and advanced toward him.

Nereo knew these were Warren and Bailey's other team members, the other three who'd been altered. Between their odd scents and their actions, he knew they intended to steal his beloved away from him. Nereo's natural instinct to care for his injured soulmate surged through him. Adjusting his hold on Warren so he could clutch him with one arm, he crouched and extended the claws of his other hand, ready to protect what was his.

"Hold," Bailey called gruffly. "Stand down, now!"

The three men froze, hesitating. An instant later, almost as one, they straightened. With their hands behind their back and their feet hip-distance apart, they stared straight ahead.

Bailey sighed deeply as he moved forward, placing himself between Nereo, Warren, and the three men. "This is Nereo

Belmonte," Bailey stated, using a hand to indicate him. "He's here to help repair your memories. It seems the process may hurt, but it is necessary." Half-turning to include Nereo in the conversation, Bailey asked, "Can you tell us what happened?"

Nereo rose back to a standing position as he retracted his claws, relaxing only a little. "I ran into something blocking my abilities," he admitted, adjusting Warren to a more comfortable hold in both arms. "It felt as if all his past, his identity, had been crumpled up into a ball, then wound with tendrils made of unnatural enzymes." Shaking his head at the strange feel of it, Nereo continued, "They definitely weren't magick, and due to the experiments and how you said you found toxins in his blood, it's definitely human-made chemicals."

"And it obviously hurt him when ye touched it?" Declan guessed, waving a hand to indicate Nereo's passed-out beloved. "Judging from his response."

Easing a hand away from Warren's arm, Nereo took a second to waggle his hand in a *sort of* motion. "I touched the threads, searching for beginnings and ends. It was when I plucked a couple to break them that it caused him agony." Clearing his throat, Nereo grumbled, "Yes, it let out a foggy memory or two, but it also caused him excruciating pain."

Lark appeared in the doorway, probably having been brought up by the commotion. "If I placed them in a coma, could you work on it safely then?"

Nereo hesitated, thinking about what he'd encountered. After a few seconds, he admitted, "The mind is such a fragile thing. I'm not certain if they'd wake up."

As Lark nibbled his bottom lip, Declan reached out and gripped his hand. He pulled his mate into an embrace, hugging him tightly. The small human's arms immediately wrapped around the alpha's waist, holding him back.

Fighting the jealousy, Nereo tore his gaze away. He saw

the way Bailey glared at the floor, his brows furrowed as if he were deep in thought. Every once in a while, his lips would pinch tight before relaxing again.

For a couple of long moments, silence filled the room.

"Permission to speak freely, sir?"

Nereo snapped his attention to the big blond male with a scar creasing his left eyebrow. It cut to the corner of the man's eye, and Nereo wondered just how close the guy had come to losing his sight. The man's blue eyes stared straight ahead, and a firm scowl turned his expression fierce.

"Yes, Miles," Bailey replied. He glanced between all three men. "You may all speak freely to me."

Miles blinked once, then focused on Bailey. "Am I to understand that this man"—he jerked his chin in Nereo's direction—"may have the ability to fix our memories? The memories lost to the experimental nerve gas we encountered on our last mission?"

As Bailey sucked in a slow, measured breath, Nereo crossed to the bed. Ever-so-gently, he placed Warren on the comforter. Unable to go far from him, Nereo settled next to him, leaning his back against the headboard.

"I *have* told you before that there was no mission," Bailey countered slowly. The scent of his frustration began to fill the room. "Doctor Winoan lied to you."

"We were debriefed by General Sackett," Miles stated, obviously still not able to let it go.

"And General Sackett lied, too." Bailey lifted his hands, palms out in placation. "I know I didn't want to believe it either, and I would be right where you are if my brother hadn't broken into the research facility where we were being held and secreted me away. That was over a year ago."

Miles's eyes narrowed as the other two men—David and Crew, according to the files Declan had shown him in the office downstairs—exchanged looks.

"Anyway," Bailey continued, trying to get everyone back on track. "To answer your question, yes. We were all illegally experimented on by Doctor Winoan and his team, with the blessing of General Sackett, and Nereo is a vampire trying to help fix what they did."

Crew slid his gaze to focus on Nereo. "Permission to ask the man a couple of questions, sir?"

Bailey nodded. "Granted. Ask as many questions as you'd like."

"How did your nails turn into three-inch talons?" Crew asked, his attention flicking over his hands. "And why do they appear normal now?"

Once more, Bailey and Nereo explained about vampires.

"Vampires are real?" David actually seemed excited by that prospect.

"We are," Nereo confirmed with a smirk. He allowed his eyes to haze back to red—a natural phenomenon giving a vampire the equivalent of infrared. They used it to track the blood within their enemy or prey, helping them choose the best places to strike or feed. After changing his eyes back, Nereo again grew his talons while opening his mouth and showing off his fangs.

"That's so cool," David whispered.

"And you can read minds, and that's how you'd hoped to fix our memories?" Miles pressed, his blue eyes narrowing just a little. After Nereo nodded once, Miles continued, "But when you tried to do it to Warren, it hurt so badly that he passed out from the pain of it."

Nereo flinched, hating that he'd caused his beloved such pain. "Yes."

"And if you put us in a coma so we don't feel the pain"—Miles turned his attention back to Lark—"we may not come out of it." He focused on Nereo once more. "Correct?"

"I'm afraid so," Nereo replied, grimacing. "If I release the bonds too swiftly, your mind could overload and be lost. If I do it too slowly, agony in a coma could pretty much do the same thing."

"I'd like to volunteer," Miles stated, returning to his earlier position, his gaze once more focused straight ahead.

"I—Wait." Bailey frowned. "You want to volunteer?"

"Yes, sir," Miles replied formally. "I am willing to take the risk."

Rubbing the back of his neck, Bailey exchanged a look with not only Nereo, but also Declan and Lark. Finally, settling on Nereo, he asked, "What do you think?"

Nereo felt his pulse spike, and he cleared his throat in discomfort. "It is his choice," he murmured softly. Quietly, he ordered, "Miles, look at me."

For an instant, Nereo didn't think Miles would obey, and he would need to have Bailey order him.

After a couple of heartbeats, Miles leveled his cold, blue-eyed gaze upon him. His expression appeared so vacant that Nereo fought against the chill that wanted to shiver up his spine.

"I can try, but this could kill you," Nereo stated baldly.

Miles immediately replied, "Better to die than live as I have been."

To Nereo's surprise, both David and Crew agreed.

"Very well." Nereo felt his stomach clench as he agreed to give the procedure a go. Focusing on Lark, he asked, "Will you prep Miles, please?"

Lark looked about as uncertain as Nereo felt, but he still nodded. "This way, please." Easing out of Declan's arms, he headed out of the room and to the right.

All four of the other altered—including Bailey—turned and followed the human.

Nereo knew he was expected to go, too. Instead, his attention shifted to his unconscious beloved. He slid his fingers over Warren's closely shorn scalp, wondering what he would look like without the military cut.

"Warren is safe here," Declan rumbled softly, moving toward him slowly. "No one here will harm him."

Nereo knew that in his head. Really, he did. After dipping his head in a nod, he forced himself to stand. He took one step, then turned back. Bending at the waist, Nereo pressed a kiss to Warren's temple.

"Rest, my beloved," Nereo whispered into his ear. "I'll be back as soon as I can."

Straightening, Nereo stared at Warren for another couple of heartbeats before heading toward the door. He stopped, making certain Declan left before him. Then he closed the door quietly behind him.

Following Declan to the right, Nereo took long deep breaths, settling his mind. He knew he would have to be swift, but not too swift. Dismantling the odd blockage would need to be done with precision and care.

When Nereo followed Declan through the third door on the left, he saw that it was set up as a small medical suite. There was an adjustable bed as well as medical equipment. Miles already lay on the bed with his shirt off and a blanket covering him to the waist.

Lark stood at a sideboard and was doing something that looked . . . doctory.

"Did I have any family, Bailey?" Miles asked, evidently deciding to trust the other male. "Wife? Kids?"

Bailey shook his head. "No. None of us did." He reached out and took Miles's right hand between both of his own. "All of us were single with little family except me. It's probably why they chose us. Few would come looking if we disappeared."

Miles nodded. "Good." Then he pulled his hand away and rested it on his toned abdominals. "I'm ready, Doc."

Lark stood at the left side of the bed and wrapped a tourniquet around Miles's left bicep. Rubbing and tapping the inside of his elbow, he must have found the vein he was looking for. He picked up the prepped needle in his gloved hands.

"You'll feel a slight pinch," Lark warned softly. After Miles had nodded, he jabbed him.

Nereo decided he'd seen enough of that. Crossing to the window, he took several more slow deep breaths. As he did that, centering his mind, he absently listened to Lark's soothing tenor.

"You're going to start feeling a little drowsy, Miles," Lark told him. "Count backward from twenty for me, and don't fight it."

Miles began counting slowly. By the time he reached twelve, his words were slightly slurred. When he reached eight, his voice came out very soft. He didn't make it to four.

Turning around, Nereo crossed his arms over his chest and rested his butt against the windowsill. He saw that Miles's chest rose and fell in slow, steady breaths. Lark was staring at a machine, checking the readings.

After several minutes where the only noise came from the beep of the machines, Lark finally looked up. "He's out. I'd like to give him another ten minutes to truly settle."

Nereo nodded. Seeing all the other men in the room, he warned, "I ask that no one interrupts me while I'm in Miles's mind. I'll also need someone to watch my back, as I'll be completely focused on him and the task I'm performing."

Lark frowned, shaking his head. "I plan to monitor Miles's vitals for the duration of this procedure. If something goes wrong, how do we signal you to quit what you're doing?" Crossing his arms over his chest, he continued, "I'm going to be monitoring you, too. What if you both need a break?"

Cocking his head, Nereo scented the concern Lark had . . . and not just for his patient.

Huh. He's concerned about me, too.

Nereo smiled, touched. "I'm in no danger, but thank you." Sobering, he hummed, thinking about Lark's question.

How could he be safely signaled?

"It'll have to be something non-intrusive but will get my attention," Nereo mused softly, tipping his head to the side. Grunting, he grabbed a rolling stool and trundled it to the right side of the bed. After settling on it, Nereo used a foot to lower the peg that would lock the wheels so it could no longer move. Then he rested his right hand on the bed near Miles's hip, palm up. Nereo pointed at it with his left hand. "If you spot something dangerous going on with Miles's vitals, tap out a steady rhythm on the pulse point of my right wrist. That will draw my attention without jolting me."

Gods, I hope so, anyway.

Lark nodded. "Okay." Then he held up a finger clip. "I know you think you don't need it, but humor me."

Smiling a little, Nereo nodded. "Very well."

Nereo didn't comment as Lark fitted him with the device. A moment later, he was hooked up to a smaller machine. Finally, Lark settled on his own stool.

Declan rested a hand on Lark's shoulder, drawing his attention. They shared a loving smile.

Nereo found his attention straying to his unconscious beloved in the bed down the hall.

To any gods who care to listen, please let this work.

Lark looked over the vitals once more, then nodded at Nereo. "We're ready."

"Okay, guys," Bailey rumbled, turning away. "That's our cue to leave. Let the vampire work."

Once everyone filed out, leaving him alone with Lark and Miles, Nereo focused on the comatose altered. After another slow deep breath, he reached up with his left hand and pried open Miles's eyelid. Then he hazed his own eyes and eased into the altered's mind.

CHAPTER FOUR

Images flashed through Warren's mind, filmy and without form.

Men in lab coats formed then disappeared. IVs appeared and disappeared from his arms. Men in uniform grinned at him. Mud coated his legs, and his body shivered from the rain pouring down upon him. The sound of gunfire stung his eardrums. The scent of steak filled his nostrils, the sizzling reaching his ears.

Wait. That last one isn't a memory.

Jerking awake, Warren jackknifed forward. He peered around wildly, searching his surroundings. Recognizing the room at the wolf shifter Declan's home, he settled.

Warren blinked slowly, staring at the ceiling. The sound of sizzling steak, as well as the scent of cooking meat, once more teased his senses. Turning his head, he spotted the window open several inches to let in the afternoon breeze.

He realized that Declan was grilling on the back patio beneath his window.

Sighing, Warren rubbed at his temples, allowing his eyelids to fall closed again. His head throbbed, and his eyes felt grainy. He tried to figure out why.

Nereo. Nereo did something to me.

Sluggishly sorting his memories, Warren recalled the best kiss of his life. Then the man — vampire — *holy shit, vampires are real* — had slipped into his brain. He'd . . . *touched* something inside him, and it had hurt like hell.

Warren couldn't ever remember a pain like that. Even

when he'd taken a bullet to his shoulder, he hadn't experienced that level of agony.

That thought brought Warren up short.

I remember something.

Except, when Warren tried to focus on it, he couldn't remember the where, why, when, or how. Still, he pulled the neck of his t-shirt to the side and peered at the puckered scar on the front of his right shoulder. After running a fingertip over it a couple of times, Warren relaxed back and once again stared at the ceiling.

Okay. So agony in exchange for a little hint into my past.

Warren wasn't entirely certain that would be worth it. Taking a moment, he tried to remember something else. Names and faces floated through his mind. Snippets of missions with his brothers-in-arms—Miles, David, Crew, and yes, Bailey, too. All of them had been there.

General Sackett had told them that on their last mission, they'd run afoul of a new experimental nerve gas. In return for saving them, they were now bound to Doctor Winoan. They'd felt that bond, too . . . a visceral need, a compulsion almost, to obey his commands.

Until that thing in my head woke up.

On the other hand, Bailey had said they'd been experimented on. Could that be true? He now recalled men in lab coats, wires and injections, needles and agonizing pain.

But that could have been from Doctor Winoan saving us, just like the general said.

Shit! I'm so confused.

Rubbing his palms over his face, Warren didn't know what to believe anymore. Well, one thing he did believe was that Nereo had given him the best damn kiss of his life. He believed that with everything in him, regardless of his memory problems.

And then he'd hurt me.

A soft knock on his door drew Warren's attention. "Yes?"

he asked, realizing his voice was rough and hoarse. Spotting the water bottle on the nightstand to his left, he grabbed it as he saw the doorknob turn. After popping the seal and taking a swig, Warren saw Lark peer in at him. "Doc?"

Lark smiled tentatively at him. "Hey, how are you feeling?" He paused with one foot in the room and half his body still hidden by the door. "May I come in?"

Warren beckoned the man as he eased to a sitting position, slinging one leg over the side of the bed. "What the hell happened?" He figured if anyone could tell him, the doctor could.

Grimacing, Lark told him, "The scientists created a block on your memories." Stepping into the room, he closed the door behind him. As Lark moved closer, he told him, "When Nereo tried to remove it, it hurt you. A lot." He grimaced, shaking his head. "He feels terrible about that, by the way. No vampire would purposefully hurt his beloved."

Resting his back against the headboard, Warren tried to process that.

He must have remained quiet for too long, for Lark asked, "How are you feeling now? Do you want any pain-relievers?"

Warren shook his head before taking another sip of water. The cool water soothed his throat, and drinking gave him a moment to gather his thoughts.

"I'm okay," Warren replied to the concern he saw in Lark's eyes. He found it interesting that his compulsion to keep his mouth shut unless ordered to by his leader had eased somewhat. He was also able to ask, "Where is Nereo now?"

"Lying down," Lark told him. "Resting."

Glancing at the sunlight streaming through the window, Warren murmured, "Right. He's a vampire." He'd made out with a vampire, and it had been the best damn kiss of his life.

Lark followed his gaze to the window and must have guessed at his thoughts. Chuckling softly, he shook his head. "Not because of the sun. That doesn't affect them."

"Then why?" Warren asked compulsively.

Why am I so worried about him?

"He spent almost four hours in Miles's brain, undoing the chemical bindings trapping his memories." Lark sighed and frowned, shaking his head. "I had to pull him out of it twice during the procedure so Miles's pulse would stabilize. I'm going to keep him in a coma for another twelve hours or so." Lark appeared worried as he murmured, "I hope that will be enough time for his mind to stabilize."

Once again confused as hell, Warren admitted, "I don't understand."

He listened as Lark explained what had been going on that afternoon while he'd slept, his own brain recovering from a sort of shock.

"So it's all true," Warren whispered, leaning his head back against the headboard. "General Sacket and Doctor Winoan used us."

Nodding, Lark softly answered, "I'm afraid so."

Every soldier had heard the stories of their brethren being left behind enemy lines, of their superiors conveniently forgetting their whereabouts to save their own skins. Hell, his own unit had needed to . . .

Frowning, Warren blinked a few times. The memory had been there and gone.

"Are you sure you don't need anything?" Lark pressed, touching his arm. "You look . . . like you're in pain."

Technically, Warren was in pain, but if he'd been on drugs and who knew what else for the past year, he didn't want more of the same.

"I'm good," Warren replied. Something else Lark said tugged at his interest. "You called me the vampire's beloved. What's that?"

To Warren's surprise, Lark's face turned a slightly pinkish hue. "Uh, right." Bobbing his head, he murmured, "I did say that, but I don't know if you're ready for the information or not."

Warren wanted to know even more upon hearing those words.

"Okay, so, every paranormal has a soul mate out there," Lark began slowly. "Someone who could be the love of their life, that they can bond with, that they'll cherish more than life itself." Touching his own chest, Lark revealed, "I'm Declan's mate. That's what a shifter calls their other half. A mate. A vampire calls his other half a beloved." Pointing at Warren, Lark stated, "And that's you to Nereo."

"Me?" Arching one brow, Warren stated, "I'm Nereo's other half?"

As Lark nodded, nibbling his bottom lip nervously as he did so, that presence in his mind rumbled happily, as if confirming everything Lark had just told him.

Okay. That's just weird, too.

"Do you know why I feel this . . . it's not a voice, really." Warren frowned, realizing how crazy his next comment was going to make him sound. "It's a presence in my head."

"That's your cat," Lark told him without any hesitation. "Since you were all part of Winoan's *experiments*" — he sneered the word, making his feelings on that clearly known — "and the fact that your inner animal recognizes Bailey as your alpha, I'm guessing you're a cheetah, too. We'll know for sure once you shift for the first time."

"I'm human," Warren countered immediately. "I don't shift."

Lark shrugged with a shake of his head. "I know it's pretty fantastical to believe, so I guess you'll just have to wait until it happens."

Warren opened his mouth, then closed it again. He didn't know what else to say. Hell, what else could he say? The doctor obviously believed his words.

Smiling widely, Lark told him, "You're definitely a lot more inquisitive now that you've met your mate and had one or two memories returned." He leaned forward and patted his wrist. "It's good to see your real personality starting to come through."

Before Warren had to come up with an answer, another knock sounded on his door. "Lark? Are ye in here?" Declan's voice came through the wood.

Lark replied, "I am."

The door opened, and Declan stuck his head in. "Hi, Warren," he greeted with a smile. "Glad to see ye awake. How are ye feeling?"

"Better, I think," Warren replied honestly. "But my mind is reeling a little at everything we've been talking about."

Wincing, Lark admitted, "I may have overwhelmed Warren with information." Moving to Declan's side, he claimed, "But he was asking questions." Lark wrapped his arms around Declan, who immediately returned the embrace, before refocusing on Warren. "You've never done that before. Not of your own accord."

Warren nodded once more. That was true. His programming—for lack of a better word—had imprinted the importance of following orders while keeping his mouth shut.

"I'm very glad to hear that, my mate." Declan dipped his head and pecked his lover's lips. Then he refocused on Warren. "The steaks are ready. Would ye like to come downstairs to eat?"

After a few seconds of hesitation, Warren nodded slowly. "I would like to try that," he told them, testing the bounds of being able to make his own decisions.

Declan smiled as he backed up a step, taking Lark with him. "There are moccasins in yer closet, if ye don't want to go barefoot. See ye down there."

Once Declan had guided Lark out, closing the door behind them, Warren eased off the bed. He crossed to the window and closed it, blocking out the coming evening's chill. Stepping off the area rug under the bed, Warren paused and stared at his bare feet.

Do I want to wear moccasins?

Yes. Yes, I do.

Warren strode to the closet and opened the door. He found the offered footwear. After donning them, he wriggled his toes, finding them lightly padded, almost like a slipper.

Comfortable.

Heading toward the door, Warren paused with his hand hovering over the doorknob. He heard the whispers of warning in his mind. He hadn't been ordered to leave his room and report downstairs.

It had been an offer.

I'm choosing to accept the offer.

Warren swallowed hard, then gripped the doorknob and turned. He opened the door and stared into the hallway. When he'd needed to use the facilities, he'd never had this problem.

Damn it. I can do this.

Growling under his breath, Warren pushed through his reservations, his conditioning that he would be punished if he acted without orders. He stepped into the hall, leaving his door slightly ajar, and turned in the direction of the stairs. Crossing to them, Warren paused at the top, once more waging a war with himself.

Warren shook his head once, then started down the stairs. Gripping the railing, he watched the activity below as he descended. Lark and Tom were setting the table. Kade was pulling food out of the refrigerator and placing it on the bar. Declan entered the dining room through the sliding glass door, holding a massive platter filled with sizzling steaks.

Warren's stomach rumbled, and everyone looked up at him. Freezing, he just managed to keep himself from going to attention.

Lark grinned widely. "Glad you could join us."

Nodding woodenly, Warren forced his feet to start moving again. He made it down the stairs, fighting against the hairs threatening to stand up at his neck. Mentally, he reminded himself over and over that he wasn't going to be punished. He no longer needed to wait for orders.

Reaching the bottom of the stairs, continuing to watch the other four men bustle around the dining and kitchen space, Warren felt something niggle at the back of his mind—something that wasn't nerves. It was almost like muscle memory, and he found himself blurting, "Is there anything I can do to help?"

Lifting his attention from where he was setting some silverware, Lark first appeared surprised. Then he grinned broadly, clearly pleased. "Will you go to that cupboard there"—he pointed at one to the left of the refrigerator—"and bring six water glasses to the table?"

Warren nodded. "Certainly." *That's easy enough, right?*

Moving around the table and into the kitchen, Warren dodged Kade, who was placing a potato dish onto the bar. He opened the cupboard and pulled down the required items, placing them on the counter. After closing the door, Warren began transferring them to the table. He felt sweat bead at his temples as he took a guess and placed one at each place setting. His gut even started cramping.

Shit! Why is this so hard? What the fuck did those assholes do to my head?

Just as Warren picked up the last two glasses, he felt strong arms wrap around his waist. Panic slammed through him. Warren snapped to attention even as the other man rested his palms on his stomach, and he prayed he wasn't about to be wrestled to the ground and hit with a shock stick.

"I'm sorry, sir," Warren shouted, his body vibrating with tension.

In the process, Warren dropped the glasses that had been

in his hands. He heard a thud as well as a shatter, but he refused to move. His best chance at avoiding a severe punishment was to stay as still as possible.

For a few seconds, nothing happened.

Then the hands on his stomach rubbed soothing circles over his abdominals, confusing Warren further. Lips pressed against his neck, followed by a cheek nuzzling him. Warren did his best to stay strong, to remain still, but a shiver of pleasure worked through him, unable to be denied.

"I'm so sorry, Warren. I didn't mean to startle you."

Warren recognized Nereo's voice, but the words were confusing him.

Why is he sorry?

After another peck to Warren's neck, Nereo lowered his hands to his waist and urged him to turn.

Taking a deep breath, Warren obeyed the urging and peered up into the vampire's concern-filled dark eyes. A glance left, then right, made him realize everyone had stopped what they were doing and were staring at him.

Embarrassment rose in his cheeks, and he desperately wished a hole would open in the floor and swallow him.

It didn't.

CHAPTER FIVE

*B*y the gods, what has my beloved been through?
Nereo wasn't certain he wanted to know the answer to that question. He also felt like an asshole for freaking him out. Of course, he'd thought Warren knew he was coming up behind him, too.

Warren did have heightened senses.

Instead, Warren must have been focusing all his attention on taking glasses to the table.

Why was that?

One thing at a time.

First, soothe my freaked-out — and embarrassed, judging by his scent — beloved.

Lifting one hand from Warren's waist, Nereo slid it up to cradle his strong, smooth jaw. "Again, I'm so sorry I startled you, beloved," he repeated softly, holding his beloved's gaze. "I didn't realize you were so deep in your head." Nereo offered his altered human a depreciative smile. "I was just so excited to see you up and about, that I couldn't resist touching you."

Warren pursed his lips ever-so-slightly while holding his gaze. "Because I'm your beloved. Your soul mate."

"Yes," Nereo confirmed, unwilling to ever deny his ties to his beloved. "You are my beloved, the other half of my soul." Cocking his head, he asked, "Do you mind telling me who shared that information with you?"

"Lark."

Turning his head, Nereo smiled at the human, who still

sported a look of concern. "Thank you, Lark. I appreciate it." Nereo refocused on Warren. "Will you accept my apology?" Touching his thumb to Warren's full lips, the lips he'd so enjoyed kissing earlier that day, he added, "Not just for startling you, but for hurting you, as well?" Grimacing, Nereo admitted, "I've never had anyone react to my trancing efforts before."

Nodding slowly, Warren replied, "It's fine. It loosened something in me." His brows furrowed, and he seemed to be searching for the right words. "I got a few memories back, and I seem to be able to make my own choices . . . if I concentrate hard enough on them."

Ah, that explained it.

"And I broke your concentration," Nereo guessed. "Which made you revert back to your . . . training?"

Warren offered him another slow nod.

"Well." Nereo began to turn, sliding his arm around Warren's waist, urging him to move out of the kitchen. "Maybe a glass of wine will help us both relax, so we can get to know each other."

Before they'd taken one step, Tom jumped forward. "Wait," he cried with lifted hands, making them freeze. "There's broken glass. Let me get the broom."

Nereo peered at the floor, seeing what Tom had noticed. While one of the glasses that Warren had dropped was still intact, the other one had shattered. Warren's moccasin-clad foot was less than an inch away from a large shard. With his own feet returned to his boots, Nereo wouldn't even have noticed if he'd stepped on one.

"Thank you, Tom." Nereo gave Kade's human a grateful smile. "I appreciate your intervention."

"I should still get the last two glasses," Warren commented absently as he stayed still under Nereo's hold. "And I don't remember if I like wine."

Smiling at Warren even as his heart saddened, Nereo told

him, "Well then, I look forward to helping you discover your interests all over again."

Warren didn't respond as Tom returned with a broom and quickly swept around their feet, clearing them a path. That seemed to be the catalyst for everyone to start moving again.

"Careful in there, Tom," Kade cautioned with furrowed brows. He appeared to be keeping a sharp eye on the human.

"I've swept up many a broken glass, Kade," Tom replied with an impish grin. "Normally because you jump me when I have a cup of coffee or glass of wine in my hand, making me drop it."

Kade growled softly, the tattooed wolf shifter's expression heating as he stared at his mate. "I can't help it if you look sexy drinking your morning coffee."

Laughing, Tom just shook his head and continued cleaning.

Warren pulled away from Nereo just enough to grab two more glasses from the cupboard. Then he allowed Nereo to guide him to the table. He placed them at the open place settings.

"Thanks, Warren," Lark replied as if nothing had happened. "I hope everyone's hungry."

"What about the others?" Nereo asked, peering overhead.

Glancing his way as he worked, Lark replied, "Bailey took off a little bit ago, heading home for a little alone time with his mate. Crew and David are still too under the influence of their *programming*." Lark said the last word with a growl in his voice. "And Miles is still in a coma."

Nereo felt his stomach clench at that news. "He is?"

Obviously catching on to his concerns, Lark assured, "I'm keeping him in it until tomorrow morning. If something happened, it'll give his brain time to recover."

Even as Nereo nodded, feeling somewhat relieved, he still heard the silent, *I hope*, that Lark hadn't tacked on.

I hope so, too.

"I'll take plates up to Crew and David before I start eating," Lark explained. "They haven't turned down medium-rare steaks, yet."

"We were trained to eat whatever was put in front of us."

Nereo touched Warren's jaw upon hearing the softly spoken comment, gaining his beloved's attention. "If you find something on your plate that you don't like, please don't feel obligated to eat it." Forcing a smile, Nereo added, "I'll find you something else instead."

"We all will," Lark assured. Frowning, he asked, "You've been here a couple of weeks. Is there anything we've given you that you don't like but ate anyway?"

Warren's eyes widened just a little as his lips parted. For all the world, the muscular soldier looked like a deer caught in the headlights. He wanted to pull Warren into his arms and soothe him, but he also knew the importance of allowing his beloved to sift through the holes they'd punctured in his training and find his own way.

So Nereo waited.

With a grimace twisting his lips, Warren revealed, "Green beans. I really don't like green beans."

"Crap," Lark muttered, shaking his head. "We've been making those every few days. I'm so sorry." His remorse was loud and clear.

Warren just shrugged, as if it truly hadn't occurred to him to refuse to eat them. Considering his *training*, Nereo knew that was true, too.

Declan returned with a second platter of steaks and placed it beside the first on the bar. "Okay, everyone. Stop lollygagging and dig in." He grinned widely as he picked up a plate and handed it to Lark. "I'll help ye with Crew and David's plates, my love."

After the pair filled the plates with massive steaks, mashed potatoes and gravy, an ear of corn on the cob, plus a heap of jello salad, they headed upstairs.

Tom was just returning from putting away the broom and dustpan, so he washed his hands first. Kade grabbed two plates and began fixing one for each of them.

Nereo found himself impressed with the size of the steaks the wolf shifter put on both plates. He wondered if Tom could actually eat all that, or if his shifter mate intended to finish what the human could not.

Probably the latter.

Halfway done, Tom crossed to Kade's side and finished making up his own plate.

"Come on," Nereo urged, guiding Warren to the buffet-style meal with a hand on his lower back. He felt the shudder that racked his altered and hoped it was due to pleasure at his touch. With the way Warren's scent had been modified, Nereo wasn't entirely certain.

I'll learn to read him in time.

"While you start filling your plate, I'm going to get us glasses of wine," Nereo told Warren. He'd been told by both Declan and Lark that they were welcome to help themselves to anything in the kitchen. He'd noticed Kade pulling beers out of the fridge for himself and Tom.

Leaving Warren to work through his own choices, Nereo strode into the kitchen. He pulled down a couple of wine glasses from the rack, then chose a bottle of red. Turning, Nereo asked, "Hey, Kade. Where does Alpha Declan keep his opener?"

With his mouth full, Kade pointed at a drawer to the left of the dishwasher.

Nereo nodded and located the item. After popping the cork, he returned it to the drawer, noticing several themed wine stoppers in there. He snagged one with the pride symbol on it. After pouring several ounces into each glass, Nereo shoved the stopper into the bottle, which he found a place for in the fridge.

Picking up the glasses, Nereo carried them to the table. "Where are we?" Nereo asked, once again focusing on Kade. He figured the pack enforcer would know which seats were Declan and Lark's usuals.

Kade once again pointed, and Nereo placed the glasses in front of the settings on the right side of the table. Kade was seated at one end, with Tom to his left. Nereo really should have just made an educated guess.

Turning, Nereo focused on the food. He saw that Warren had chosen a medium-sized steak as well as a heaping pile of mashed potatoes doused with gravy. His beloved seemed to be hesitating over the jello salad. Warren frowned at it, as if he wasn't certain if he wanted to try the red concoction containing small chunks of fruit or not.

With his instinct screaming at him to ease his beloved's concern, Nereo turned and grabbed the fork from his place setting. He stood at Warren's side and scooped up a small amount of the jello salad. Then he held it to Warren's lips.

When Warren met Nereo's gaze, he told him, "If you like it, take some. If you don't like it, then don't."

A flash of relief entered Warren's hazel eyes, and he opened his mouth.

Nereo slid the utensil into his beloved's mouth. As he watched the man he soon wanted to make his lover wrap his lips around the tines, he suddenly felt a wash of jealousy for the damn fork. Pushing it aside, Nereo pulled the fork free and waited, wondering what the verdict would be.

After swallowing the mouthful, Warren picked up the scooper and placed a healthy dollop of the stuff onto his plate.

Smiling, Nereo returned his fork to the table and began preparing his own plate. He'd just finished when Declan and Lark returned. With a gentle touch to Warren's back, Nereo urged him to the table.

Warren sat.

After Nereo had taken a big bite of his own mashed pota-toes and gravy — *yum* — Warren followed suit.

Not a lot of talking ensued, unless it was a request to pass the salt, pepper, or ask whoever was up for another beer or to fetch the bottle of wine. As it turned out, Warren did enjoy the wine, and Nereo even opened a second bottle. He ate heartily, and seeing that pleased Nereo, even though it was a com-pletely irrational feeling since he hadn't made any of the food.

They were halfway through the meal when the throaty rumble of some high-end vehicle reached Nereo's ears. Cock-ing his head, he listened, trying to place the motor. When he did, he couldn't help but turn his attention to Declan.

"I have to ask. Which of your pack-members drives a *Por-sche?*" Nereo had always been a *Corvette* guy, but *Porsche* def-initely made some pretty cars.

Scoffing, Declan replied, "That would be Prier. Even while building his new identity, he had to have his favorite type of car."

Lark tipped his chin up. "Not that he and Kajika aren't al-ways welcome, but were we expecting them?"

Declan shook his head. "Maybe it's good news."

"Are we expecting news?" Lark quipped. "What was he looking into?"

"Whatever he wants to look into," Kade replied with a laugh.

Snickering, Lark nodded.

Nereo had heard that Kajika was the wolf pack's head en-forcer, and his mate was human, but Prier was still known as the pack fixer, of a sort. The man was a hacker, bombmaker, and, if some of Vince's stories could be believed, an ex-assas-sin.

The front door opened, and two sets of footsteps entered the home before it closed again.

"Hey, perfect timing, Injun," a lithe man commented as he

sauntered into the room. "I'm starved."

Lark smirked at the pair. "You know the door's always open to you. Help yourself."

"Oh, look at that," Prier stated as he grabbed a plate, which he handed to Kajika—a tall, muscular shifter who appeared of Native American descent. "The vampire fixed one of them already. Sweet."

"Eh." Kade lifted his hand and waggled it back and forth in a so-so gesture. As he lowered his hand to pick up his beer, he focused on Warren and offered, "No offense."

"Kajika, Prier," Declan began as the pair pulled up chairs. "This is Council Enforcer Nereo Belmonte, and the altered is Warren Berger." Declan then introduced the pair who'd joined them.

While cutting his steak, Prier asked, "So what does *eh* mean?"

"It means I pulled a couple of threads to help a few memories surface," Nereo answered the human. "Unfortunately, it was rather agonizing to him." Resting his hand on Warren's thigh, he murmured, "And it still makes my heart ache knowing I caused you pain, my beloved."

"Beloved?" Prier grinned broadly. "You bonded, yet?"

"Not yet," Nereo replied, although he sure hoped he could get to that soon . . . as in perhaps after dinner.

"What's bonding?" Warren asked softly, glancing around warily. "What's that mean?"

Lark's jaw sagged open. "Oh. Oh, dang it. I did totally skip that part, didn't I?"

Prier gave Lark a scandalized look. "Dude! How could you skip over the best part?" Shaking his head, he leaned an elbow on the table and pointed his fork at Warren. "So, you bond when you fuck. Our new fangy friend here will sink those lovely teeth into you and drink while reaming your—"

"Prier, I think he gets the picture," Kajika cut in smoothly, resting his tanned hand over Prier's wrist. With a wide smile, he focused on Warren and finished, "Let's just say, it's an amorous experience."

After popping a bite of steak into his mouth, Prier nodded.

Nereo appreciated that Prier didn't talk with his mouth full. The human had already said quite enough. When Vince and his friends had offered warnings about the pair, he hadn't believed them.

He did now.

Focusing on Warren, Nereo opened his mouth to reassure him . . . somehow.

Warren beat him to it. "You intend to bite me?"

Snapping his mouth shut, Nereo cleared his throat and shifted in his seat. He dipped his head in a quick nod. "Yes, but you'll enjoy it."

"How can getting bitten be enjoyable?" Warren didn't look convinced, and his frown and scent betrayed his unease and disbelief.

See, I am beginning to read him.

Fortunately, it was Tom who answered before Prier could finish swallowing and open his mouth again.

"I know it seems counter-intuitive," Tom said with a wry smile. "But believe it or not, getting bitten by your paranormal lover will make you" — he cleared his throat, his cheeks turning pink, and he even lowered his voice as he finished — "orgasm."

Warren's brows furrowed, and he stared at his plate for a few seconds before muttering, "Can't remember the last time I did that."

All Nereo's blood went straight to his cock.

Oh, holy fuck.

CHAPTER SIX

W arren couldn't believe he'd just blurted that out. *Damn.*

Once again, he wished for that hole that didn't appear.

Fortunately, Lark came to his rescue. "Well, that makes sense, since you're just starting to get back a memory here or there." He smiled brightly at Warren while adding, "And I'm certain Nereo here will be happy to fix that problem."

"As soon as you wish," Nereo rumbled, his voice gruff.

Warren noticed a hint of red gleaming in the vampire's eyes. Recalling what had happened last time Nereo's eyes turned red, he quickly returned his focus to his plate.

"Hey," Nereo crooned, touching his chin. "I'm a patient vampire. Bonding can wait."

When Warren looked back at the male, he was relieved to see the redness gone. "It wasn't that," he admitted. Upon seeing Nereo's questioning look, he told him, "Your eyes were starting to go red. The last time that happened, you entered my mind and" — instead of saying he'd ended up in agony, he hesitated before finishing — "I passed out for a while, and I don't want to do that again."

Nereo must have somehow guessed what he was actually thinking, for he flinched. "My eyes will turn red for a number of reasons," he explained. "Using my mental abilities is only one of them."

"What are the other ones?" Warren asked.

"They'll turn red when I prepare to feed or fight," Nereo told him, obviously being honest. "When my eyes turn red, or haze, as we call it, it's sort of like infrared. It allows us to track the blood pathways. We know where to bite to give maximum pleasure, or where to strike to do optimal damage."

Warren nodded slowly. "Okay." Peering at Nereo, he asked bluntly, "Was your eyes changing because you were thinking about fucking?"

"Well, I would much rather we make love, but yes." Nereo's lips quirked in a small smile. "I was thinking about engaging in the horizontal tango with you."

Barking a laugh, Warren grinned. "Okay." What else was he supposed to say?

Nereo's eyes widened. "Okay?"

Realizing how Nereo must have taken his response, agreement to bond, Warren quickly asked, "After we bond, what's expected of a vampire's beloved?"

Sobering, Nereo nodded. "Right. Well, once a vampire meets his or her beloved, they can never drink from anyone else ever again, so I would need you near," he explained slowly. "And I work for the Vampire Council, which is based in Savannah, Georgia."

"You'd expect me to move there," Warren guessed.

Nereo dipped his chin in a single nod. "That would be ideal, yes."

Warren didn't have much in the way of memories, and he still struggled to make choices. He could sense that inner presence urging him to accept, to bond with the vampire. If it was a cat, as Lark believed, would that make a difference?

"They tell me I've been experimented on," Warren began, working through his thoughts, trying to decide how he felt on the matter. Seeing Nereo nod, Warren continued, "If that's the case, and Lark is right, I might change into a cat at some point."

Saying those words out loud sounded bat-shit crazy to Warren, but he understood that these people were trying to help him, help them all. Bailey had been their unit leader. The uniforms in his hazy memory told him that. Then this inner presence switched his loyalty from Winoan to Bailey in the blink of an eye.

"There isn't a question in there," Nereo commented.

Right.

"How does it work if you're a vampire and I turn into a cat?" Warren asked, working his mind around the issue. "Will I attack you?"

"Absolutely not," Declan answered, putting down his knife and fork. "A shifter is completely cognizant while in animal form. Bailey is, and you would be, too."

Warren licked his lips, thinking on that. "Cognizant. As in self-aware?"

"Correct," Declan confirmed. "When I'm a wolf, I know my family, I know my friends, and I know my pack-mates." He reached over and threaded his fingers with Lark's. "I would never attack those that I care about. As a wolf, I would protect my mate with every fiber of my being." With a confident smile, Declan told him, "You would be the same."

"When do you change forms?" Warren asked curiously. "On the full moon?"

"Well, we've done a piss-poor job of explaining shifters to these guys," Kade muttered gruffly. Sitting back in his chair, he rubbed one palm over his goatee while tapping the forefinger of his other hand on the beer bottle he held. "Once a shifter learns how to change their shape, they can do it at will. No full moon required." Shrugging one shoulder, Kade added, "We do like to gather on the full moon to barbeque and run as a pack, but that's for camaraderie, not because we have to."

Nodding once more, Warren thought about that. "I would need to live with you because you need my blood." He met Nereo's gaze. "Would other vampires be okay with that?"

To Warren's surprise, Nereo grinned broadly. "Okay with

it?" He chuckled deeply. "Hell, every unbonded vampire within a hundred miles will be jealous as fuck to discover that I've met and bonded with my beloved." Turning in his chair, Nereo cradled Warren's near hand between both of his own. "Warren, finding your Fate-given beloved is the greatest gift any paranormal can receive. Nearly all of us strive to meet that special someone." Lifting Warren's hand to his lips, Nereo added, "And now that I have, I will do everything in my power to fill your life with joy." He hesitated a second before adding, "Even if that means I give up my position so we can live wherever you want."

Oh, that sounds like – "Am I right in assuming that this is like a marriage?"

"Not *like* a marriage," Nereo countered. "This is *more* than a marriage. This is a bond deep down in our souls."

Warren rubbed the back of his neck with his free hand as he peered around the table at everyone. They all sported serious or earnest expressions. Well, all except for Prier. When Warren met that man's gaze, he waggled his eyebrows.

Strange man.

Finally returning his focus to Nereo, Warren saw the expectant gleam in his dark eyes. The vampire wanted him. Still, he had to warn, "I'm not fixed, yet. What if I never am?"

Nereo just smiled at him with a look that appeared almost . . . loving. "I don't care if you're never fixed." He lifted one hand to make air quotes. "You're mine, and you're perfect just the way you are."

"But you're here to fix us," Warren countered, confused. "I heard about Miles and the coma."

Sighing deeply, Nereo frowned at where he held Warren's hand for a few seconds. When he lifted his gaze again, his expression had turned grim. "Removing what the scientists did to you was for your benefit, to help free you from their influence." Nereo squeezed Warren's fingers once more as he told him, "If we didn't try to figure out some way to return some of your faculties to you, giving you the right to reject an order, then we'd always run the risk of them capturing you and your friends and using them for their own nefarious purposes once more."

Warren accepted that. Nereo wasn't saying he needed to change to be good enough. Instead, he was trying to help Warren become a better version of himself for the sake of safety.

"Okay." Warren nodded while smiling at Nereo. "I'll bond with you."

"Got champagne, Alpha?" Prier quipped.

Declan scoffed, stating, "We'll toast after they've completed their bond."

Warren could see the blaze of heat and lust ignite in Nereo's eyes. After all, they began to turn a smidge red. That time, he didn't turn away from the vampire. Instead, Warren leaned forward and kissed him.

While Warren had originally meant for it to be a soft peck, a promise for things to come, Nereo grabbed his nape and quickly deepened the kiss. He thrust his tongue into Warren's mouth, licking and tasting. Warren felt that presence in his mind growl with delight, and he responded in kind, giving as good as he got.

A wolf whistle rent the air, reminding Warren where they were — sitting in the alpha's dining room.

Nereo groaned into his mouth before breaking the kiss. A sheepish smile curved the vampire's lips as he glanced around at everyone. Then Nereo shrugged, jumped to his feet, and swung Warren into his arms.

Warren gasped as Nereo streaked up the stairs faster than his mind could easily process. The vampire shouldered into his room and used a foot to kick the door closed. When they reached the bed, Warren thought he would be tossed upon it. To his surprise, he was carefully lowered onto the mattress, and Nereo rested one knee upon it to place a gentle kiss to his lips.

A knock sounded on the door, and Warren groaned. Nereo growled, whipping his head to look in that direction. The door opened, but no one entered. Instead, someone — Kade, judging by the tattoos covering the appendage — stuck in their arm and wiggled something.

Nereo huffed a laugh, got up, and retrieved it.

"Thanks," the vampire muttered.

A low chuckle reached Warren before Nereo shut the door and locked it.

"Almost forgot one of the most important things," Nereo told him, returning to the bed.

When Nereo placed the tube on the nightstand, Warren realized it was lube.

Yup. Definitely important.

Crunching up, Warren whipped his shirt over his head and tossed it to the floor. At the same time, he toed off his moccasins. After shucking his sweatpants, he turned his attention back to Nereo.

Warren groaned softly in appreciation. Even though the vampire had seemed to have a hell of a lot more clothes on, he'd still managed to get nude just as fast, if not faster, than Warren. Licking his lips, Warren admired the miles of muscular, olive-toned flesh on display.

With Warren's attention snagging on Nereo's probably nine-inch erection jutting from his neatly trimmed bush, he couldn't help but lick his lips. "You're stunning," he muttered as he watched a bead of pre-cum ooze from Nereo's slit. "Want to taste you."

"Who am I to say no to such a generous offer," Nereo replied, easing onto the bed to hover half over him. Leaning down, he thrust his tongue into Warren's mouth and gave him a slow, languorous kiss before lifting away. His eyes once more gleamed with shades of red in his irises. "But only if I can return the favor while opening your ass."

Warren's ass clenched as muscle memory pressed into his brain. "Yessss," he hissed, more than on board with that.

He might not be able to guess how long it had been, but something in him told him how fantastic it would be.

Taking him at his word, Nereo shuffled their positions on the bed. He lay Warren under him as he levered over him, his knees to either side of his head. Nereo's mouth hovered over his hard and aching cock, and Warren let out a long, low moan when his new lover blew a warm breath over his leaking crown.

"Yeah, I like those sounds," Nereo muttered right before he opened his mouth and took Warren to the root.

Barking a cry, Warren arched. Pleasure erupted through him as Nereo applied tight suction as he drew off. His gut clenched, and his breath stuttered in his chest.

"N-Nereo," Warren whined as a shudder worked through him.

Popping off Warren's dick while rubbing up and down his thigh soothingly, Nereo crooned, "Right here, my beloved. Right here." Then he swiped his tongue all around Warren's cap.

A drop of moisture hitting his cheek yanked Warren out of his pleasure. Snapping open eyelids he couldn't remember closing, he spotted Nereo's thick erection hovering over his face. As he watched, another bead of pre-cum pooled on the head, threatening to fall.

Unwilling to waste another drop, Warren did his best to ignore the perfect suction on his own prick — at least, for a few seconds. He grabbed a pillow and shoved it under his head, putting himself at the perfect angle. Then Warren gripped the base of Nereo's thick rod, tipped it down, and wrapped his lips around the male's swollen flesh.

The grunt of pleasure that vibrated Warren's erection shot

a bolt of satisfaction through him. He lapped at Nereo's crown, teased under the cap, and sucked strongly as he bobbed along his length. Adding grunts and hums of his own, he shared the sensual vibration with the vampire.

Warren reveled in the taste of Nereo's pre-cum, enjoying every drop he managed to suck out of him. Focusing on the masculine flavor filling his mouth helped ease him back from the edge. His desire to pleasure his lover curbed his balls' need for release.

Then, to his shock, a sharp prick jolted through his dick. Even as Warren realized Nereo had bit him, the sensation morphed into unimaginable pleasure. His balls tightened, and his orgasm slammed through his system.

Moaning around Nereo's thick length, Warren flooded the vampire's mouth with his seed. His lover continued to suck on him, and his mind floated with bliss. Rocking and trembling in Nereo's hold, Warren lost all sense of which way was up.

Warren couldn't have said how long it took him to return to himself. He finally began to regain his faculties only to find Nereo had turned around on the bed. The vampire rested between his thigh, levering half over him. A smug smile curved his lips.

"There you are, my beloved," Nereo crooned, grinning like the cat that ate the canary. "Gods, you taste delicious." Dipping his head, he pressed a light, too-short kiss to Warren's lips. "Will enjoy your succulent taste forever."

Dragging a few brain cells together, Warren muttered, "Y-You bit my dick."

"Mmm-hmmm," Nereo replied, not in the least bit repentant. "You almost had me tipping over the edge." He winked. "I had to distract you somehow."

"By biting my dick." Warren would forever deny the squeak in his voice.

Nereo lowered his head and whispered huskily into Warren's ear, "And you loved it and will want me to do it again and again."

Warren opened his mouth to deny that claim, but then he recalled how hard he'd come.

Why the hell would I deny myself that pleasure?

After swallowing hard, Warren admitted, "Yeah."

Easing up, Nereo continued to grin. "Now, I'm going to make you come all over again."

Warren didn't know how that could be possible after such a strong orgasm. Then he realized something he hadn't noticed before. Nereo had several fingers in his chute, massaging and stretching him.

Sighing, Warren pushed into the touch. "Oh, hell yeah."

Still grinning, Nereo eased his fingers free and lined up his already lubed-up cock.

When Nereo pushed into him, Warren gripped Nereo's shoulders and welcomed the vampire deep inside his body.

CHAPTER SEVEN

Nereo moaned roughly upon feeling Warren's tight, velvety channel envelop his cock. Once he'd pressed as deeply as he could go—his groin pressed flush to his beloved's cheeks—he forced his hips to still. Not only did Nereo need to give Warren a moment to become accustomed to his girth—he wasn't a small man, by any means—but what he'd told Warren had been so damn true.

His beloved altered's blowjob had pushed him so close to the edge. Only by distracting the man had he been able to stop the rise of his orgasm. Of course, the mixture of blood and semen had nearly caused the same reaction.

Fortunately, Nereo had pulled his dick free of Warren's inviting mouth just in time. Their first time together, he wanted to bury his seed in his beloved's ass. He wanted to bond them, connecting their life-lines for all time.

Nereo had taken advantage of Warren's blissed-out state, which had allowed him to stretch him swiftly.

And now, I'm in my beloved, the other half of my soul.

Nothing had ever felt so exquisite.

"Move," Warren pleaded, clenching and releasing around Nereo's flesh. "Please, move."

"Anything you want," Nereo whispered, before capturing Warren's lips.

As Nereo once again explored Warren's mouth, enjoying the trace flavors of himself on his tongue, he eased his hips back before thrusting forward again. Starting a slow, lazy rhythm, Nereo felt every nerve ending in his cock light up.

Warren encased him in the most delicious squeezing heat, and he knew he would never get enough of it.

Feeling Warren's fingers dig into his shoulders, Nereo growled softly into his mouth. He pushed his arm under his altered's torso as he pressed his weight into him. Reaching between them, he gripped Warren's once-more straining erection.

Oh, yeah.

Knowing he didn't have much left in the way of self-control, Nereo sped up his ruts, jacking Warren in time with his thrusts. He adjusted the angle each time until he felt that telltale jolt go through his lover beneath him. Humming into Warren's mouth, he picked up the pace.

Warren broke the kiss on a whine, his face going to the crook of Nereo's shoulder. More than happy with that, and with the feel of Warren mouthing sucking kisses up his neck, Nereo mirrored him, doing the same. He pounded into his lover as he sought out the vein he wanted. His mouth watered with the prospect of tasting more of Warren's heady life-fluid.

"Nereo!" Warren cried into his ear, the sound of his pleasure bouncing across the walls.

In the same instant, the cock he jacked pulsed and twitched in his hold, coating his fingers with cum.

Moaning his own pleasure, Nereo sank his cock in as deeply as possible and rode the crest of his orgasm. His body shuddered and twitched as he poured his fluids into the man who was quickly coming to mean everything to him. Unable to deny his instinct, Nereo sank his fangs deep into Warren's flesh.

When Warren's blood oozed up around his teeth, Nereo sucked and swallowed. He drew more and more of his beloved's succulent ambrosia into him, making his mind spin with the ecstasy of it. Nothing had ever tasted or would ever taste as wonderful as his beloved.

Groaning softly, Nereo finally eased his fangs free and

licked over the wounds, closing them and leaving a lovely bonding scar. He smiled at the mark before kissing it lightly. Nuzzling Warren's neck with his cheek, he sighed deeply . . . then gasped.

Pain flared through his neck and shoulder as Warren sank his teeth deep into Nereo's flesh. In the next instant, the sweetest of tingles danced across his skin. Nereo's nipples beaded, and his gut clenched. His balls felt as if they turned inside out as a fresh orgasm bowled through him, sending him soaring.

Nereo moaned Warren's name as he felt his beloved suck at his neck. The sensation seemed to transfer straight to his cock, drawing more and more cum from his already drained testicles. The pleasure and pain mixed, and his eyes nearly rolled to the back of his head.

When Warren eased his teeth from Nereo's flesh and licked over the wound, Nereo dropped unceremoniously on his lover. He felt drained, but in the best of ways. His body continued to experience light shudders of aftershocks, and he feared he would never be able to move again.

"Gods, Warren," Nereo mumbled roughly, his lips pressed to his lover's solid chest. "You're amazing."

Warren heaved a deep sigh, and his voice came out gruff. "I'm pretty sure I should say that about you." Rubbing his hands up and down Nereo's back, he mumbled, "Holy fucking shift, Nereo. Will it always be that intense?"

Forcing his weight on his left arm, allowing him to push off Warren a little so Nereo could meet his gaze, he smiled at him. "Sex is always better between those Fate blesses," Nereo told him. "But that surpassed any expectation I could possibly have imagined." Smiling crookedly at Warren, Nereo added, "And I'm an almost two-centuries old vampire."

"Damn," Warren murmured, his hazel eyes widening in disbelief. "Two centuries?"

Carefully easing out of Warren, Nereo groaned softly before flopping to the left. He cuddled up to his slightly smaller lover and rested his head on his right shoulder. "Yeah. We can live upward of five centuries barring injury or accident . . . or war."

Feeling Warren tense beneath him, Nereo tipped his head up a bit to look at his lover. He saw the frown and rubbed his cheek over his chest, trying to soothe him. That also smeared Warren's cum into his skin, which smelled amazing.

"What's wrong?" Nereo murmured. "Please talk to me."

"You're going to outlive me by centuries."

Upon hearing Warren's hushed comment, Nereo realized there were still a few gaps in his beloved's education. "No, my beloved," he countered, touching his chin to get him to meet his gaze. "We are bonded. Our life threads are now one. We will age together, so you'll live as long as I, and vice-versa."

Warren held his gaze for a moment, blinking a few times as he processed that. "So, if the army came for me and killed me, you would die?"

Ah, my beloved has a pessimistic streak. We're going to have to work on that.

"I'm just being realistic," Warren told him sadly.

Nereo recalled the telepathic link that developed between a vampire and his beloved.

Something else to explain.

That time, Nereo made certain not to project his thought.

"Warren, if you were to die, I wouldn't want to live anyway," Nereo told him gently. "You're my heart and soul. I wouldn't want to live without that." Then he growled softly as he added, "And if the military attempts to come for you, I will tear out their throats and bathe in their blood."

Nereo wasn't a Vampire Council enforcer for no reason.

"That sounds . . ." Warren's words trailed away as a smile flickered around his lips. "Actually, there's a part of me that really likes the sound of that."

Chuckling, Nereo nodded. "Good." Rocking up, he pecked a kiss to Warren's lips. "Now, come on. Let's go get cleaned up before we stick together." Even as Nereo eased away from Warren, he winked at him, "Not that I don't think that would be a lot of fun."

Warren chuckled as he shook his head.

Nereo hoped to be able to get his solemn altered human to make that noise often.

When the morning light teased across the backs of Nereo's eyelids, he turned his head and hid his face in Warren's neck. He tightened his hold a little where he spooned behind his lover. His prick gave a half-hearted flop, and he had to smile.

Yeah, a half-dozen rounds throughout the course of the night would even wear out a vampire.

Hearing Warren's breathing change, Nereo kissed the back of his neck. "Morning, my beloved," he murmured.

Warren grunted and pressed back into his hold. "How about we stay just like this . . . all morning?"

Nereo liked that idea very much. "Do you think we can get them to bring us meals?" he asked, the corners of his lips twitching. "Like room service?"

"They are for my team mates," Warren pointed out. "Why not for us?"

"Good point." Nereo began sucking up a mark on Warren's neck. His flesh just tasted too delicious not to mark.

Grunting, Warren tipped his chin up, offering more room.

Just when Nereo's cock began to thicken, and he was giving serious thought to another round after all, a knock sounded on their door.

Groaning, Nereo released Warren's flesh. He pulled the blanket higher up their torsos and called, "Enter."

Alpha Declan strode into the room. Beta Dixon was with

him. Both men sported serious expressions.

"Something's happened." Nereo glanced between them, and he felt his stomach clench. "Is it Miles? Did he not make it?"

"It's something else," Declan told him, quickly assuaging his concerns. "Lark just removed the chemicals keeping Miles under a short while ago. He doesn't expect the man to be able to wake up for another couple of hours."

Relief flooded Nereo, and he blew out a breath. "Then?"

Declan and Dixon exchanged a glance. The alpha focused on him again and told him, "Get cleaned up. I need ye both in my office as soon as possible." He smiled tightly as he added, "We'll have coffee and breakfast waiting."

Then they filed back out, closing the door softly behind them.

"That sounded ominous," Warren stated, concern in his voice and scent.

"Yes, it did," Nereo agreed. Pushing the blanket down, he took a second to kiss Warren's shoulder over his claiming scar before easing from the bed. "Only one way to find out, so let's not borrow trouble."

Warren nodded as he followed him from the bed.

While Warren pulled sweats and a shirt out of the dresser, Nereo placed his duffel bag on the bed. After their shower the previous evening, he'd started to make his way down the stairs wrapped only in a towel. He knew shifters didn't care much about nudity.

To Nereo's pleasure, Kade had already fetched his duffel bag and tossed it up to him, allowing Nereo to return to the room without going outside. He pulled a pair of jeans and a polo from the bag and yanked them on. After adding socks and his boots to his feet, Nereo finger-combed his hair.

They quickly took turns in the bathroom in the hall before making their way down the stairs.

Nereo figured they reeked of sex, but he'd decided Declan's urge for speed meant the others would just have to deal
with it. Something serious had to be going on. Otherwise,
there was no point in interrupting a newly bonded couple on
the morning after their mating.

Keeping his fingers threaded through Warren's, Nereo
urged him down the hall to the study. His beloved seemed
uncertain and edgy. Nereo guessed his conditioning was beginning to kick in.

Now that they were bonded, Nereo hoped that would
begin to fade a bit, but only time would tell.

As soon as Nereo opened the office door, the blessed scent
of coffee flooded his senses. He led the way to the sideboard
and quickly filled a mug. Turning to Warren, he asked how
he liked it.

His answer of black didn't surprise Nereo, so he handed
over the cup, then poured a second one. To his own, he added
a bit of cream. After taking a tentative sip, Nereo hummed in
appreciation and took a larger swallow.

Peering at everyone over the rim of his cup, Nereo took in
serious expressions, furrowed brows, and full plates of food.
He couldn't imagine what could put a shifter off their food,
so he knew it had to be serious. Deciding to wait on making a
plate for himself, Nereo slung his arm around Warren's waist,
the driving need to keep his beloved close surging through
him.

"Do you want food, my beloved?" Nereo murmured into
his ear.

Warren shook his head, and Nereo wondered if his altered
was picking up the tension as well.

*Probably. Regardless of conditioning, he'd still been a soldier for
many years.*

As Nereo guided Warren to an open sofa, he met Alpha
Declan's gaze. Beta Dixon rose from his seat and cracked the
window. Enforcer Kajika remained stoic, although his mate

grinned broadly. Enforcer Kade's lips twitched.

There were a couple of other men in the room that Nereo didn't know, and his vampire nature began to make him feel edgy with so many shifters in one place, him with a beloved not at one hundred percent, and him with no back-up.

Damn it. What the hell is going on?

"Please, try to relax," Alpha Declan urged, lifting a hand in placation. "We would never harm you or yer beloved."

"In my head, I know that," Nereo replied as he and Warren eased onto the sofa cushion. Using his mug to indicate everyone, because he sure as hell wasn't going to release Warren, he stated, "But with so many gathered, it's natural to feel concern."

Alpha Declan nodded. "Understandable. Just remember, ye're a guest in my home. Any attack against you would be an attack against me." Then he pointed at a redhead and stated, "Enforcer Manon" — then a guy with light-brown hair — "Enforcer Gracen."

Nereo dipped his chin to each man in turn.

"I'll get straight to the point," Alpha Declan began, cradling his mug between his palms as he rested his elbows on his knees. "We have a contact in the CIA, remember?"

Nodding slowly, Nereo vaguely recalled how Alpha Declan had called a gathering to share that the CIA knew about paranormals.

"When we took down the facility where we found Warren and the others, we asked the CIA for aid," Declan revealed. "It was time they started cleaning up the human threat themselves, since they're so adamant that we keep to the shadows." Shaking his head, Declan grumbled, "Not that I have a problem with that, but it's the human scientists that risk our anonymity the most, so the CIA should be held accountable to stop them."

That made sense to Nereo.

"So, anyway, the CIA took in all the scientists, their data, and any animals that were real animals," Declan continued.

"After I made a copy of all material, of course," Prier cut in with a grin. "Can't have any secrets between us and the CIA, right?"

Declan dipped his head in acknowledgment, although he didn't outright condone the human's antics. "And we took the shifters." Declan picked up as if Prier hadn't interrupted. "Along with that, we took Bailey's men."

Nereo still wasn't seeing the problem. "Makes sense."

"Well, General Sackett has contacted the CIA," Declan revealed. "He's making claims that he had an undercover team on the ground there when the CIA raided the place, and he wants his men released." Declan pinned his gaze on Warren. "He wants you and yer team members."

CHAPTER EIGHT

Warren sat frozen in shock, his coffee cup cradled between his palms.

Doesn't this just fucking figure. Something starts to go my way, and now I'm going to get pulled back in.

"Not a chance in hell," Nereo roared, leaping to his feet. He stood in front of Warren, as if he intended to fight every man in the place. "Warren is mine. I'll take him and his whole group. My people will protect them if you can't."

Alpha Declan once again lifted his hand in placation. "That's not what I'm saying at all, Nereo," he claimed. "Please, sit down. Right now, I'm just sharing facts."

Nereo growled as he perused the room.

Reaching up, Warren gripped Nereo's belt loop. He tugged lightly. Even he could see that every shifter in the room was tensed, ready to spring into action if his vampire did something stupid.

When Warren tugged a second time, Nereo turned and focused on him. Forcing a small smile, Warren tipped his chin toward the sofa. Still growling, Nereo retook his seat. He slung his arm back around Warren's shoulders and clutched him close. Glaring over the rim of his coffee mug—Warren was impressed he hadn't spilled the thing—Nereo took a deep gulp.

"So we're on the same page," Alpha Declan continued, focusing on Warren. "Agent Craigson and his director, a fella named Agent Reiste, doesn't want General Sackett or any of his associates to have ye back, either. They've managed to put together a pretty strong case against him, but they need a bit more time to implement it. A bit more digging." Relaxing back in his seat, Alpha Declan added, "When they take Sackett down, they want to make certain they tie up all loose ends this time, and I would very much like for them to be able to do it." With a tight smile, the alpha added, "Besides, not only are ye shifters now, but ye're mated into the paranormal world. That makes all of ye ours."

"So, what's going to happen?" Warren wondered why Alpha Declan had even decided to let them know. *Oh, shit.* "Does he know where we are?"

"We believe Sackett has his suspicions," Beta Dixon revealed. "We've spotted a few questionable characters in and around town recently, but we haven't engaged them. We're just watching, and so are they."

After taking a sip of his own coffee, Warren gave in to the urge and pressed tighter into Nereo's side. "God, I just want to be left alone," he whispered, shaking his head. "Out of curiosity, how's he making a play for us?"

"Well, according to Agent Craigson, the general says ye were investigating that facility because they thought there may be a terrorist connection," Alpha Declan explained. "He sent yer group to attempt to facilitate an arms deal."

"Uh, that's not what we do." Warren shook his head. "We don't engage in operations on our home soil."

"Evidently, Sackett has someone inside homeland backing him up," Dixon grumbled, crossing his arms over his chest. "There's some kind of special task force documentation, but we all know that's bullshit."

Warren couldn't even begin to wrap his mind around it, so he didn't even try. Instead, he asked, "So, is there a plan?"

"Yeah." Prier's smile appeared a little creepy. "Keep you out of enemy hands and kill anyone who tries to take you away."

Declan rubbed at his temple while Dixon hid a smirk behind his coffee mug. A couple of the enforcers rolled their eyes, one openly chuckled, and Prier's mate pecked a kiss to his cheek.

Prier beamed at Kajika and waggled his eyebrows. "I love how talk of bloodshed get's you all ramped up."

"I just like watching you kick ass, babe," Kajika responded gruffly.

Warren didn't know how to take that couple, so he dismissed them in favor of focusing on the alpha.

"So, anyway," Declan began slowly. "I'm obviously not a fan of having the military creeping around my pack lands, no matter the reason." His deep gray eyes narrowed as he mused, "We need to make it look like we never brought ye here."

"How?" Dixon asked bluntly.

Declan sighed. "That's the question. Isn't it?"

"I have an idea that you're not going to like," Prier offered.

"If it's anything along the lines of me giving my beloved to the CIA to pass on to General Asshole, so you can track another facility," Nereo cut in, glaring at the guy. "Then forget it."

"I told you that you wouldn't like it."

It had obviously been a good guess.

"Not a snowball's chance in hell," Alpha Declan countered vehemently. "No more putting my people in the line of fire. I'm done with that bullshit."

"Then we play defense while we wait for the CIA to get their shit together," Dixon stated, rubbing his hand over his bald scalp. "We need to spread the word. Alert every member of the pack. They need to know that trouble is in the area."

Declan nodded. "No one runs alone, and we'll implement a curfew for the pack."

Warren sighed before whispering, "You're putting your

own people in jail just to keep us safe?" Guilt surged through him.

Shaking his head, Declan pinned him with a hard stare. "I would do this for any members of my pack. A pack protects its own, no matter how new the member." He narrowed his eyes. "And don't try to do anything stupid. That's an order."

Knowing he wouldn't be able to go against the blatant statement even if he had been able to figure out a way out of the woods, he nodded. "Yes, sir." Besides, one of his team was upstairs incapacitated. No way in hell would he go anywhere without Miles.

Nereo squeezed his shoulders and pressed a kiss to his temple.

We all knew you were thinking about it.

Narrowing his eyes, Warren stared at Nereo. He wondered if he'd really heard his lover's voice in his head.

Yes. It's one of the things that's unique to a vampire bond. Nereo pressed his lips to Warren's temple again, his lips lingering. *We can speak telepathically to each other, but only if we direct the thought to each other.*

Warren nodded just a smidge, wondering if he thought that was cool or creepy.

Nereo chuckled softly, so he must not have kept the thought to himself.

I'll teach you. It just takes some practice.

Once again, Warren nodded. Then he refocused on the problem at hand. There were men under General Sackett's command searching for him and the others in this area. His greatest fear was that if the general did get hold of him, he would be reprocessed, losing all memory of Nereo.

And if Nereo loses me, he'll die. He can't drink from any other.

That was completely unacceptable.

Warren racked his brain, trying to think of some way to help.

I need my goddamned memories.

But how?

"Does anyone know what base I'd been stationed at?" Warren asked, during a lull in the conversation.

"I can find out for you," Prier offered. "Why?"

"What if General Sackett disappeared?" Warren mused.

With a deep sigh, Declan admitted, "I'm sorry to say that we've tried that once before. You all remember General Jackson Parker?"

"Gods, that guy was a real douche," Kajika commented with a snort.

Warren didn't remember the name, not that that meant much. "What happened to him?" he asked curiously.

"Well, he separated fated mates," Kajika began.

"Killed his son's shifter mate, so he went a little crazy," Prier added with a grimace.

"And was going to sell his infant shifter daughter to the highest bidder," Alpha Declan told him with a growl in his voice. "We rescued her, kidnapped him, and enacted shifter justice on the asshole. Since he knew about the paranormal world, he fell under our purview."

Manon snapped his fingers before saying, "I talked with Magdaline just last month. Little Amelia is doing fantastic in their pride."

Declan smiled. "Good. I'm glad to hear it."

"Okay, so kidnapping the general is out," Warren mumbled.

"Actually, no it's not," Nereo cut in. "I think it's time the vampires got involved in this." With a hard smile, he added, "We *are* working together often enough these days. If we don't nip it in the bud, it could end up biting us in the ass eventually."

Nodding, Declan asked, "Who should I call about it?"

Nereo shook his head. "No. *I'll* make a call." Perhaps to soften the denial, he added, "These people are after the bonded beloved of a Vampire Council enforcer. They're after one of *our* own, too."

Declan nodded once more. "Thank ye, Nereo. If ye don't mind keeping me posted, I'd appreciate it." After Nereo dipped his chin in confirmation, Declan swept his gaze over the group. "Okay, people. We have our plan. Stay vigilant, and keep each other safe."

As everyone began filing from the room, Nereo focused on Warren. "Let's fix a couple of plates and take them up to our room."

Warren nodded. "Okay."

They waited until most of the others had filed out, then rose to their feet. Warren stayed close to Nereo as they headed to the buffet. As they filled their plates, Alpha Declan joined them, topping off his cup of coffee.

"Are ye doing okay, Warren?" the alpha asked, clear concern in his tone. "Please know we never intended for ye to be placed in harm's way . . . again."

Offering the alpha a smile, Warren told him, "Your people saved us at great risk to yourselves. We know you'll do your best." Glancing around the room, he softly asked, "Why wasn't Bailey at the meeting? Why me, instead?"

Alpha Declan chuckled as he replied, "We called him. Clayton answered. I guess he'd just left to visit his brother and had forgotten his phone." Shrugging, Declan added, "Clayton told us he'd give Ronan a call. The pair are devising ways to keep in contact with their sister since their mother turned out to be a homophobe." Declan shook his head sadly. "After everything that family went through, and she can't just love her damn sons. I just don't understand people."

"That's too bad," Warren murmured, frowning.

"Anyway." Declan patted him on the shoulder. "I'll bring him up to speed once he gets here. I know he talked about swinging by this afternoon to see how you and Miles are coming along."

Warren picked up his plate, ready to spend a little more alone time with his vampire. "Thank you again, sir."

While Warren knew everyone called him Alpha or Declan, he just couldn't seem to get his mind around that title.

"Ye're welcome."

Fortunately, Declan didn't seem to mind.

Turning toward a waiting Nereo, Warren headed that way. Since both their hands were full between plates and mugs, he couldn't reach for Nereo's hand the way he wanted. Instead, Warren brushed his shoulder into his vampire's, expressing affection in another way.

Nereo cast a smile his way, then led the way to their bedroom.

While Warren knew it was a borrowed space, he still liked thinking of it as theirs. He enjoyed the idea of it being all their own. Recalling that Nereo lived in Savannah, he tried to recall if he'd ever been in that area.

He couldn't.

Maybe it will come back to me.

As they set their plates and mugs on the nightstand, Warren asked, "Would you be willing to pluck at a few more of the strings in my mind?" While it had hurt like hell, now that he was processing things better, he wanted more of that.

Nereo swung around and quickly wrapped him in his arms. The big vampire clutched him close, rubbing a palm up and down his spine. "But it was agony for you," he whispered into Warren's neck.

The concern and sadness filling Nereo's tone nearly took Warren's breath away. He'd heard his lover apologize several times for what had happened, and it occurred to him that never once had Warren said it was okay. Taking the opportunity, he did so then.

"I don't blame you for what happened, Nereo," Warren told him. "You were trying to help, and in a way, it did. I've started to recall things here and there." Teasing his fingertips through Nereo's long hair at the base of his skull, Warren admitted, "If you're willing, I'd like to try again. Maybe, now that I know what to expect, it won't be so bad."

A guy could hope, after all.

Nereo groaned softly. They remained still for several moments, wrapped up in each other's arms, touching and petting with no intent to take it further. Warren enjoyed the embrace, which felt just as intimate as some of the things they'd done during the night.

Finally, Nereo nodded against Warren's neck. "If that's what you want, my beloved."

"Thank you," Warren whispered back. "I know you hate hurting me, and I don't make the request lightly." Easing back, he pecked a kiss to Nereo's lips. "After breakfast."

Giving Warren a look filled with relief, Nereo smiled and nodded.

True to his word, after breakfast, Nereo prepared to peer into Warren's mind once more. With the recollection of the agony at the forefront of his mind, Warren relaxed on the mattress with Nereo beside him. Threading his fingers with his vampire's, Warren held his gaze.

Warren watched Nereo's eyes bleed to red. A second later, agony fired through his entire body. Opening his mouth, he managed to choke back the scream. Instead, he let unconsciousness take him.

CHAPTER NINE

Sitting beside his unconscious beloved, Nereo wrestled with his guilt. He understood why Warren had asked for another mind session, even if it did cause him agony. Except, Nereo was causing that pain to his beloved, and it hurt his heart to do it.

Nereo did his best to hide that from Warren so he could give him what he seemed to so desperately need.

Anything for you, my beloved.

Picking up his phone from the nightstand, Nereo called Vince. The other enforcer answered on the second ring. "Hey, Nereo. How's it going out there?"

As Nereo stared down at Warren, who seemed to have slipped into a peaceful slumber, judging by the look on his face, he revealed to his friend, "I found my beloved."

Vince barked a laugh. "Well, damn, my friend. Congratulations." Before Nereo could respond, Vince quickly added, "In a wolf shifter? Who?"

Nereo shook his head. "In one of the altered humans. And thank you." Sighing, he smiled at Warren. "He's absolutely stunning. So damn kind but serious." Lowering his voice, Nereo added, "These guys' minds have been seriously fucked with, Vince, and the guys who helped do it are still after them. I need help."

The other vampire's growl came through the line. "Someone is after your beloved? Who? We'll deal with them."

Relief filled Nereo that he had someone at his back. "Thank you." Then Nereo quickly filled Vince in on everything that had happened. "I'm still waiting to hear from Lark about Miles. I'm worried about him."

Grunting, Vince confirmed, "Dealing with anything in the mind is so fucking dangerous."

"It is." With a rueful sigh, Nereo added, "So much for a simple look-see assignment, huh?"

"Eh, you got your beloved out of it."

Nodding, Nereo returned his focus to Warren, keeping vigil over him. "I hurt him, Vince," he murmured, sadness filling his voice. "Not once, but twice."

"Twice?" Vince sounded shocked. "What do you mean, twice?"

Nereo muttered, "He asked me to work on his mind a bit more, even though it hurt him. How could I say no to my beloved?"

Groaning softly, Vince replied, "You couldn't. Of course, you couldn't. It's not in our nature to deny a request from the other half of our soul."

"What if Warren asks me to keep doing it?" Nereo's voice broke at the end of the sentence. "I'm not certain I'm strong enough to keep doing that to him."

"Nereo," Vince rumbled, chastising gently. "You'll do what your beloved needs. Fate wouldn't pair you with him if you couldn't do that for him."

Taking a deep breath, Nereo nodded before tipping his head back to rest against the board behind him. "Thanks, man."

"Don't thank me," Vince replied with a soft chuckle. "I learned that shit from Frankie."

Nereo chuckled softly, thinking of Vince's wolf shifter mate. Upon first meeting the man, most would think he was a bit dim. Nothing could have been further from the truth. True, sometimes it took Frankie a little longer to process information, but that could happen to anyone who'd been on the losing end with a logging truck. On top of that, Frankie had taught Vince how to love.

Anyone who could manage that was brilliant in Nereo's book.

"Speaking of Frankie and his pack, we're going to head out there," Vince declared. "If trouble is stalking his pack, I know he'll want to be there."

"Where's Donny?" Nereo asked, referring to Vince and Frankie's young son. "Is he here with Reb?"

Reb was Frankie's older brother, and due to Vince traveling so much, they sort of co-parented. If the job Vince was going on wasn't safe, they left their kid with Reb and his mate, Daithi.

"He is, which is another reason we'll be out," Vince told him. "I'll have this wrapped up in a few more days."

"That was quicker than you expected," Nereo commented. The whole reason Vince had asked Nereo to check on the altered was because he'd thought he would be stuck at the coven, ferreting out the troublemakers, for at least another two weeks.

Vince laughed. "Yeah, well, Frankie's nose led us right to the deceptive morons. Can't hide from my wolf."

Smiling, Nereo murmured, "I look forward to one day meeting Warren's cheetah. I bet he'll be spectacular."

"They haven't shifted, yet?" Vince sounded surprised.

"I think it's taken them this long for Bailey to even convince them that what they think happened isn't the truth," Nereo explained. "And no. None of them have shifted, yet."

"Well, good luck to them when it happens." With a wince in his tone, Vince added, "Hope that doesn't hurt like hell, too, for them."

Nereo groaned. "Didn't even think of that." Shaking his head, he frowned at his sleeping beloved. "These poor guys sure have had it rough." His tone darkened as he spat, "Ass-hole scientists."

"Speaking of them, I'm going to give a few of the others a call," Vince told him. "Spread the news. I think Caspian will be in town soon, too. We can set up a meeting with Council Elder Vespa. I bet he'll give us the green light on acquiring General Sackett and extracting the information we need from him." Chuckling darkly, Vince added, "One way or another."

Nereo sure as hell hoped so. "Thank you. Please keep me posted."

"You got it, buddy," Vince replied. "No one goes after a vampire's beloved and gets away with it."

Then Vince disconnected the line.

After returning his phone to the nightstand, Nereo slid down the bed and sprawled next to his lover. He curved around him with a sigh and cuddled close to him. Gently rubbing Warren's chest, Nereo allowed his eyelids to slip closed.

Before long, the sound of Warren's deep even breaths lulled Nereo to sleep.

"No, they're both asleep."

The deep voice tugged at Nereo's consciousness.

Lark's melodious tenor replied on a soft laugh, "Well, they were up most of the night."

Embarrassment threatened to flood Nereo, but he ruthlessly pushed it back. After all, every paranormal who'd found and claimed their beloved—or mate—understood the intensity and joy.

Cracking an eyelid, Nereo spotted the door swinging shut. He was damn tempted to let it go and go back to sleep. Still, he was interested in what the pair had wanted or needed.

"I'm awake," Nereo whispered, thinking the deep voice had belonged to Bailey.

Just as Nereo had suspected, the door swung back open,

and Bailey and Lark peered in at him.

Bailey swept his gaze over the still-sleeping Warren. "Wear him out, huh?" he teased softly, a grin curving his lips, and he waggled his eyebrows. "I'm happy for him."

Grimacing, Nereo turned a little so he could eye the guys better while doing his best not to disturb Warren. "No, he's sleeping off the effects of another mind session."

Lark winced. "Really?"

"Why?" Bailey scowled. "Why would you do that to him?"

As Lark scolded, "Hush," Nereo felt a fresh stab of guilt fill him.

Sighing in discomfort, Nereo told them, "He asked me."

Bailey's features twisted in understanding and commiseration. "And you couldn't say no, even though you didn't want to hurt him."

"Exactly," Nereo confirmed. "He's my beloved." Just as Vince had told him, he found himself reiterating, "If I can give it to him, I'll do it, even if the pain he goes through breaks my heart."

"And that's what makes you a fantastic mate for him," Lark stated with a sage nod.

"What time is it?" Nereo asked. "Is Miles awake, yet?"

A troubled expression crossed Lark's face. "I'm sorry. He's not. And I think it's around three-thirty."

Humming, Nereo realized that explained the grogginess. Their short nap had turned into the rest of the morning and half the afternoon.

Guess we really did go at it all night long.

That thought caused a smile to tug at the corners of his lips, and he spotted the knowing expressions on the guys' faces.

Clearing his throat lightly, Nereo asked, "So, is there another reason you poked your head in to check on us?"

Lark shrugged. "You missed lunch."

"Ah."

As a vampire who'd just fed on his shifter mate's rich and

succulent blood, he wouldn't feel any ill-effects from a missed meal or two. That probably couldn't be said for Warren, however. Nereo made a mental note not to allow his beloved to make skipping meals a habit.

"I think the other guys want to try the painful option," Bailey revealed, crossing his arms over his chest. He scowled at the floor. "They see the slight change in Warren, and while some of it could be the fact that you've bonded, they still want a go at it." Lifting his gaze to him, Bailey asked, "If you're okay with giving it a go with them."

Nereo nodded slowly. It was the whole reason he'd made the trip out there. "Give me a few minutes to pee and clean up, and I'll meet you in whichever room you want."

"Thanks, Nereo," Bailey replied. "I can't imagine this is any fun for you, either."

Shrugging one shoulder, Nereo kept his thoughts to himself on the matter. With mental manipulations, he often learned far more than he ever needed to know about a person. Vampires had to learn to compartmentalize early on in their lives.

After the pair had exited, Nereo carefully eased off the mattress. He pressed a kiss to Warren's nape before heading to the bathroom. After a quick wash-up, Nereo glanced up and down the hall.

Lark stood in the doorway of a room and beckoned to him.

Nereo spotted one of the altered lying on the bed. From delving into Warren and Miles's memories, he knew him to be Crew. Crossing to the bed, he met the man's dark-brown eyes.

"Hello, Crew. I understand you asked for me?"

Crew glanced at Bailey, who murmured, "You can talk to him."

"Yes," Crew replied. "I wish to try."

"And you are aware that this is extremely painful?" Nereo

needed to confirm it.

"Yes," Crew responded again. "I heard Warren's scream."

Yeah, that'll haunt me for a while, too.

Nereo sat on the edge of the bed and took the brown-haired man's hand. "And you are willing to endure that agony for a chance at regaining your memories? Gaining your free will?"

Crew blinked once, twice, then once more stated, "Yes, I wish to try."

"Fair enough," Nereo murmured. "Relax your mind. I'm only going to pluck a few this time around," he warned. "We'll see how you respond."

After another slow blink, Crew held his gaze. "Thank you."

Nereo nodded again. He turned his attention to Bailey and warned, "You may want to get ready to hold him down." Another thought occurred to him. "Or do you have a strip of leather for him to bite down on?"

Bailey hesitated an instant, then quickly removed his belt. "Open your mouth," he ordered as he folded the length in half. "Bite on this, and if you feel yourself losing consciousness, just go with it."

Once Crew confirmed the order, Nereo hazed his vision and slipped into the man's mind.

Two minutes later, Crew lay unconscious while Lark checked his pulse.

Nereo rubbed his palms over his face. "Damn," he mumbled. "These guys have already been through so much. I hate that I'm causing them additional pain."

"You're helping them," Bailey told him, patting his shoulder. "Or trying to. Do you need to rest before seeing David?"

Shaking his head, Nereo rose to his feet. "No, let's get this over with," he told the other altered around a rueful smile.

Fifteen minutes later, Nereo slipped back into the bedroom he shared with Warren. He quickly stripped naked and slid under the covers. Curling around Warren, he allowed the feel of holding his beloved in his arms to soothe his guilt.

For the next four days, Nereo issued one brain scan session on each of the men. While they each showed signs of progress, Warren's was the most significant. Nereo put it down to the bond between them.

While Warren was now able to walk freely around the house with very few relapses unless he was startled, Crew and David struggled. They persevered through encouragement from the shifters. Everyone always did their best to be understanding of their limitations.

The one they still worried about was Miles. Nereo slipped into his brain every day, checking his activity. The man seemed to be sleeping, and Nereo had witnessed a number of dreams—nightmares really. He didn't tell the others, but he worried Miles might have ended up too far inside his head to ever pull himself out.

Lark ended up intubating him in order to feed him fluids and nutrients.

Nereo knew the doctor would never give up as long as there was brain activity, and Nereo respected him for that.

The activity in town seemed to die down, but no one was willing to consider that the danger had passed. After all, according to Declan, Agent Craigson told him that General Sackett was still making a nuisance of himself.

After seven days, Vince and his friends, plus their beloveds, arrived in town.

Nereo watched in amusement as Caspian's little albino bunny shifter beloved—Casey—flung himself into Prier's arms. The human caught him and swung him around, grinning. He even waggled his eyebrows playfully at Caspian, who issued a longsuffering sigh.

The barbeque that night was loud, with plenty of bawdy tales tossed in. David and Crew only made it through half the evening before their nerves and conditioning forced them to retreat to their rooms. Even Warren's scent gave away his discomfort, but he stuck close to Nereo and stayed outside.

Nereo actually counted that as a win, and when ten o'clock rolled around, he was more than ready to retire himself. Keeping Warren tucked close to his side, he guided his beloved back into the house.

After slowly stripping his altered human, Nereo made slow sweet love to his beloved, putting the other men's shenanigans out of his mind for the night.

CHAPTER TEN

Warren waited patiently for Nereo to finish working with Crew and David, delving into their minds and snapping more of the bonds that kept their memories from them. He cringed when he heard Crew's shout of pain. Normally, Nereo took care of Warren first, so he didn't have to hear his friends' cries.

Telling Nereo that he wanted to be held afterward, Warren had convinced him to do the others first. As he listened, the firmer his resolve became. His vampire never uttered a complaint, but Warren knew—Nereo hated that he caused any of them pain.

Nereo had allowed a stray thought to slip through their bond a time or two.

No more secrets.

After Crew fell silent, there were soft murmurings and footsteps.

Warren knew his lover headed to David's room, and the cycle started all over again. Loud, pain-filled groans filled the air. A bark of surprise echoed down the hall. Even a whimper escaped the usually stoic David.

Both of his team members were making progress. Not like Warren, he realized, but still . . . progress.

And it's all because of my amazing vampire.

With the arrival of Nereo's friends, they'd offered to take a turn, but Nereo had declined. He had a system. He knew what to look for, how to get in, do what needed to be done, and out again with minimal effort and pain. Nereo had a system in place that worked, so they stuck with it.

Warren was no fool. He'd seen the looks of concern Vince and Frankie had given Nereo. They'd whispered into his ear and patted his back. His friends were worried about him.

So am I.

When David fell silent, Warren relaxed on the bed under the covers. He waited patiently for his vampire. The knob turned, and Nereo stepped inside.

For a second or two, Nereo didn't meet his eyes. When he did, Warren spotted the strain in his eyes before he could hide it. Then Nereo smiled and moved toward him.

The only difference between him working with his friends was that Lark and Bailey accompanied him. When Nereo worked with Warren, he was alone. Warren had originally guessed that it had to do with Nereo being territorial.

Now, Warren felt certain there was another reason.

Nereo hated hurting his beloved, and he didn't want anyone to see him doing it.

"Hello, my vampire," Warren greeted softly.

Warren liked the way Nereo's dark eyes lit up when he called him that. Nereo smiled at him, his gaze filled with warmth.

Sitting on the side of the bed, Nereo took his hand between both of his own. "Are you ready?"

Quickly shaking his head, Warren told him, "Not yet." Squeezing his vampire's hand, he urged, "Take off your clothes, and come under here with me."

With his free hand, Warren lifted the blanket.

Nereo's eyes widened as he swept his focus over his naked body. Heat immediately filled his expression, only to be quickly banked. Still, Nereo did as Warren had urged.

After stripping and folding his clothes, leaving them on the nearby chair, Nereo crawled into bed with him.

Wrapping his arms around Nereo's neck, Warren pulled

his vampire flush against him. His lover didn't resist, pressing against him, flushing their bodies as they lay on their sides and ate at each other's mouths. Kissing Nereo was always like sticking his finger in a light socket, but in a good way. It lit Warren up on the inside and heated from the inside out.

When breathing became paramount, Warren broke the kiss and turned his face into his neck. He breathed in his vampire's masculine scent. Declan was helping him differentiate between odors, allowing him to read a person better.

Currently, Nereo was aroused with a hint of concern. When his vampire asked, "Is something wrong?" Warren knew he'd read his lover correctly.

Shaking his head, Warren pulled back and smiled up at Nereo. "Nothing's wrong. I just wanted to feel you against me when I tell you that I don't want any more mind-mending sessions."

Nereo's dark brows shot up, surprise etching across his features. "Really?" His brows slowly lowered. "Are you certain? Did I hurt you too badly last time?"

"I'm certain," Warren assured, massaging Nereo's shoulders, trying to work out some of the tension he felt under his palms. "And no, you didn't hurt me. It's actually been getting better every time." Either that or Warren was just getting used to the pain, but he didn't offer that idea. Instead, he offered, "I know you hate hurting me. Hate hurting any of us."

"But if it's what you need, then I'll do everything in my power to help," Nereo told him, not denying the hating giving pain part in the least. Teasing his fingertips along Warren's jaw, he murmured, "I want you happy."

"What makes you happy?" Warren countered.

"You." Nereo's gaze held a calm certainty. "Any way I can get you."

"Well then, good," Warren replied with a grin. "Because this is how you're going to get me. I'm good now. Really good."

Nereo peered into his eyes, staring as if searching for something. His eyes narrowed when he asked, "Are you doing this just to make me feel better?"

Warren chuckled as he shook his head. "No. I'm doing this to make me feel better. I don't like you hurting me any more than you like hurting me." Squinting, Warren quickly replayed that in his head. "Yeah, that's right." Threading his fingers through Nereo's thick, dark locks, Warren added, "Besides, I'm in a good place right now." Touching his fingertips to Nereo's lips to stop him from speaking, he smiled at him. "I know I still don't have all my memories, and I'm okay with that. I remember enough. Some good, some bad."

Glancing toward the wall, Warren mused, "I know those men are my family as well as my friends. I recall their strengths and weaknesses, how we've all had each other's backs for almost a decade." Warren returned his focus to Nereo and traced a finger around his full lips. "Yes, I hope you'll still help them, but I'm good now. I'm right where I want to be, because of you."

"You were uncomfortable at the barbeque last night," Nereo pointed out. "Were there too many people barking orders?"

Warren chuckled as he shook his head. "No, there were just too many people. Period. I haven't felt the urge to listen to any orders but yours and the ones my cat have urged us to follow when Bailey gives a command." Seeing Nereo's worried frown, Warren told him, "But that feels completely different than the kind of compulsion I used to experience when following Winoan's commands." Shaking his head, he added, "It's hard to explain, but it's different. I don't feel that way anymore."

Nereo hesitated a second before nodding slowly. "If you're certain."

"I am." Warren pushed against Nereo's shoulders, pleased when he immediately acquiesced, rolling to his back. "And I want to thank you by sucking your cock."

Chuckling softly, Nereo murmured, "Who am I to deny that request?"

"Oh, it really wasn't a request," Warren told him, pushing the blanket down the bed, baring his sexy vampire for his pleasure.

Nereo had a thick build and muscular frame, perfect for climbing all over without Warren fearing that he would hurt him. The fact that he was a vampire with increased strength and speed helped in that, too. The experiments had left Warren with increased strength, too, and with Nereo, he knew he would never have to keep himself in check.

Pushing thoughts of anything but the gorgeous man sprawled in their bed from his mind, Warren focused on Nereo's quickly filling dick. He bent and lapped at the crown, enjoying the way it continued to harden, as if stretching toward his mouth for more attention. Warren was happy to give it that attention.

Opening his mouth, Warren wrapped his lips around Nereo's crown. He relished the grunt that escaped the bigger man, a sound so full of need. His vampire's hips jerked a bit, as if he was barely resisting thrusting deep and sinking his cock further into Warren's mouth.

Wanting Nereo out of his mind with lust, Warren began to do all the things he'd learned his vampire loved. He sank deep only to pull back up and release him. After blowing across his head, Warren tapped his slit with his tongue. His reward was a very tasty dollop of pre-cum.

Warren swallowed Nereo's dick to the root, lodging his vampire's cock head in his throat. After swallowing around it twice, he sucked hard as he pulled back up. Bringing his hands into play, Warren cradled Nereo's balls and gave them a gentle roll. At the same time, he wrapped his fingers around the base of his shaft and began offering mini-jacks. Then Warren teased his tongue into the sensitive flesh beneath his crown.

Nereo's rough groans and grunts were music to Warren's ears. He loved the way his heavy cock jerked and twitched in his hold. The nearly constant dribble of pre-cum caused his taste buds to sing.

Feeling Nereo's hand on his head, Warren peered up at him through his lashes. His vampire stared down at him with a heavy-lidded gaze. His eyes were hazed red, and he panted between parted lips.

Smiling around his mouthful of flesh, Warren admired his lover's nearly blissed-out expression. He enjoyed the feel of Nereo's hands on him. They weren't pulling or pushing. Nereo just touched him, as if he needed to feel him to remain grounded or he would fly away.

Warren shifted the way he cradled Nereo's ball sack, reaching with his middle finger. Pushing against the soft skin directly behind them, Nereo sucked in a sharp breath. His nostrils flared, and his fingers twitched.

Humming, Warren pressed there again . . . and again . . . and that was all it took. Nereo cried Warren's name as he filled his mouth with his seed. Swallowing swiftly, Warren drank every drop his vampire could give him.

As soon as Nereo stopped shooting, he crunched up and gripped under Warren's arms. He dragged him up his body and claimed his mouth in a wet, sloppy kiss, driving his tongue deep to share the last few drops of his cum. Warren opened wide and accepted the tongue-fucking.

At the same time, Warren rocked his hips, rubbing his hard-on against Nereo's spit-dampened groin. The smooth glide felt exquisite on his sensitive flesh. He moaned into Nereo's mouth.

So close.

Now.

Hearing his vampire's demand through their link coincided with Nereo's fangs sinking into his flesh. The spark of pain was nearly instantly soothed by his tongue sweeping over his skin around his embedded teeth. Then his vampire sucked.

Warren moaned and shot. His balls poured his cum into the space between them in bliss-inducing spurts. He trembled and shook in Nereo's hold as his vampire fed, drawing his blood from his veins.

Oh, Nereo. Sighing, Warren felt Nereo slide his fangs from his neck. *So good. Always so good.*

Always. Nereo licked his mark closed. Then he turned his head and kissed Warren once more. *I taste delicious on your tongue.*

Chuckling into Nereo's mouth, Warren grinned at the metallic tinge to his flavor. *I taste delicious on yours.*

Nereo broke the kiss and grinned. "We'll taste delicious together."

"Always," Warren agreed. Settling on top of his vampire, he used his foot to snag the comforter and pull it up enough for him to grab it with his hand. With a sigh, Warren relaxed, rubbing his cheek over Nereo's broad chest. "We don't have to be anywhere, do we?"

"Nowhere but right here in each other's arms."

Warren sure liked that idea.

The *pop-pop-pop* noise yanked Warren out of a sound sleep. He jerked his head up and stared at Nereo in shock. "That was—"

Another round followed.

"Yep." Nereo helped Warren to his feet, only hissing a bit when their skin stuck together. "I knew it had been too damn quiet."

"How do you think they found us?" Worry and fear rolled

through Warren in equal measure. He was finally moving on with his life, and now they were trying to draw him back in.

"Money can grease a lot of palms or just the wrong thing said at the wrong time," Nereo stated, grabbing his jeans from the chair and beginning to yank them on.

Warren started to reach for his sweats, but an odd sensation worked through him. His vision swam for a second, and he grabbed the side of the dresser to steady himself. Feeling Nereo grip his elbow, Warren realized black spots had appeared on his vision.

"Warren?" Nereo held him close. "What's wrong?"

"I-I'm not sure," Warren stuttered. Another shudder worked through him, and beads of sweat popped out on his brow. His joints suddenly ached, and he barely stayed on his feet. "I-I think I-I'm going to be sick."

Nereo shook his head. "On your knees, my beloved," he countered. "I think you're about to shift."

"Now?" Warren whined. "But—"

Once more, gunfire sounded in the distance, and a low growl erupted from Warren's throat. He couldn't ever remember making that noise before.

"The fact that we're being attacked probably triggered it," Nereo told him, sounding way too damn reasonable. "Your new nature means you'll want to be in your strongest form when in a battle. That's with teeth and claws. The ability to jump and climb."

"B-But what about you?" Warren whispered. The last word came out a long groan as his body started twisting and turning in some very uncomfortable ways.

"I'm a vampire, remember?" Nereo told him. "And our mind-link will still allow us to speak." He rubbed his fingers down Warren's back soothingly. "Stop fighting it, my beloved. Just let it flow."

Trying to do as Nereo urged, Warren collapsed on the floor

and let the cat take him.

CHAPTER ELEVEN

Nereo wasn't entirely certain he was giving Warren the right advice. Hell, he wasn't a shifter. Still, he'd heard Frankie talk about it once or twice, and that seemed to be what the big wolf had been saying.

As soon as Warren slumped to the floor and focused on breathing deeply, the shudders appeared to lessen, so Nereo hoped he'd said something right. Rubbing down Warren's spine, he did his best to soothe his beloved. Nereo desperately wanted to go to the window and peek out, but he refused to leave Warren's side as he went through his first shift.

"You're going to be fine, my beautiful shifter," Nereo crooned, watching the skin ripple beneath his palm. "Just let it flow."

As Nereo watched, Warren's body reshaped, and his limbs realigned. Fur sprouted on his body, beautiful sun-burnished orange with black spots all over him. The long tail begged to be stroked, but Nereo resisted . . . barely.

Once the shift was complete, Warren's cheetah flopped to his side. His chest rose and fell swiftly, and his pink tongue lolled from between powerful jaws full of sharp teeth. The beast looked exhausted, as if it had run a marathon.

Nereo rubbed down Warren's back and reached for him through their bond. *You with me, Warren?*

This feels so weird.

Sliding his fingers up, Nereo scratched behind the cat's rounded ear. *Oh, I don't know.* He couldn't help but tease his shifter. *In this form, you have hair on your head. I like it.*

The cat chuffed, which Nereo took for a laugh. He also opened his eye and peered at him with one golden orb.

"Hello, Warren," Nereo murmured, smiling at his massive cat. "We really need to head downstairs and figure out what's going on. Do you feel up to it?"

While Nereo hadn't been able to hear the gunfire over the sounds of Warren's first shift, now that they were quiet again, the *pop-pop-pop* sound returned.

Pushing to his feet, Warren attempted to stand. He staggered a bit as he took his first few steps. Then he seemed to find his rhythm and began padding toward the door.

Nereo grabbed his shirt as he passed the chair. After opening the door, he pulled it on. He glanced left and right, but the hallway was empty.

"Think we should check your friends?" Nereo asked.

Good idea.

Nereo led the way, reaching Crew's door first. A look inside told him that the man still rested from their mind session. Closing the door, Nereo hurried to David's room and found him in a similar state. Finally, Nereo reached Miles's medical suite.

To Nereo's utter shock, he found Miles sitting up in bed, gagging as he removed the tube down his throat. He hurried forward to assist. By the time they got it removed, spit and drool dripped down the big man's face.

Miles just grabbed the corner of the blanket and wiped it away. Then he snagged the base of the needle and yanked it from his arm. The blond tossed it in the vicinity of the now squealing machine.

"Fucking thing," Miles snarled. "Turn the damn thing off."

Nereo didn't actually know how, so he found the plug and pulled it out. By the time he turned around, Miles had his feet on the floor, but he didn't seem able to stand on his own. He leaned heavily on the bed, panting from exertion.

"Why the hell do I feel weak as a kitten," Miles grumbled,

scowling at Nereo.

"You've been in a coma for over a week, Miles," Nereo told him, crossing to his side. "Do you remember who I am?"

"Yeah." Miles's cheeks pinkened a little. "I remember everything. You were in my brain."

Nereo nodded. "That's right." He didn't like the way Miles wouldn't look at him, but there wasn't much he could do to reassure him that he would never tell a soul about the things he'd seen. "Come on. We need to find the others and figure out what the hell is going on out there."

Wrapping his arm around Miles's waist, Nereo urged him to lean on him.

"Is that Warren?" Miles stared at him in interest. "I'm gonna turn into one of those at some point, too, aren't I?"

"Yes." Nereo didn't see the point of beating around the bush. "I'm sure you'll look very nice." Upon hearing Warren's warning growl, Nereo quickly added, "Not as nice as my Warren, but I'm sure someone will appreciate it."

"Har, har," Miles grumbled, stumbling almost drunkenly. "Where's Crew and David?" he asked, changing the subject. "They already downstairs?"

"They're unconscious," Nereo answered without thinking. Upon seeing the alarm flood Miles's face, he quickly amended, "Not injured. When we didn't know what was going on with you and the coma, we didn't do the same thing with them. We were trying something different."

"Gunfire woke me up," Miles muttered, giving him the side-eye. "What kind of different?"

Nereo shook his head. "Now really isn't the time."

"Okay."

Warren reached the end of the hall first.

Be careful, my beloved. Worry flooded Nereo that he wasn't by his cheetah's side.

Damn it. There's soldiers down there. Warren backed up a

couple of steps. *I think they saw me.*

"Hey, there's one upstairs," someone hollered. "You two. Go get it."

Yup. They spotted you. Nereo rested Miles against a doorframe, lifting a finger to his lips in warning.

The recalcitrant soldier rolled his eyes.

Nereo focused on the corner where the stairs ended. A second later, a soldier came barreling around the corner. Without even bothering with his claws, Nereo grabbed the end of the gun he carried and shoved the barrel toward the ceiling. Even as the guy began to unload a few rounds, Nereo punched him in the throat. The man went down like a ton of bricks, sprawling on the floor.

When Nereo turned, he spotted the second soldier flat on his back. Warren's large paws stood on his chest. His fangs were bared just inches from the man's face. The guy's weapon had been forced wide and pointed toward the far wall.

Nicely done.

I was a soldier, you know.

Nereo would bet that if Warren were in human form, he would have scowled at him. Yes, sometimes he forgot that his healing altered had once been a badass soldier. His beloved should never be in danger again.

"Hey, did you guys get it?" a voice called from below.

Before Nereo had to think up a response, Alpha Declan hollered, "Ye know, ye really shouldn't just wander into someone's home in the middle of the woods." The alpha's voice carried from outside, and Nereo frowned.

What the hell?

Nereo glanced at Warren, but he knew his lover wouldn't know anything. Hearing a groan from behind him, he turned and saw Miles sliding down the wall. His sweatpants-clad butt hit the floor with a soft thump, and he grunted. A second later, Miles yanked the gun from the man Nereo had laid out. He quickly checked the magazine before slapping it back into place. Panting softly, Miles offered Nereo a crooked smile.

Evidently, the man felt much better now that he had a way to defend himself.

That was fine by Nereo.

Miles has always hated when we get into a situation he wasn't prepared for. His cheetah stared at him steadily. *Miles loves control.*

Having been inside Miles's brain, Nereo knew that. He also knew *why* the man felt that way, but he banished those thoughts. He smiled at Warren and offered a simple response. *I know, my beloved.*

"Come out of my home with yer hands up, and we'll consider letting yer soldiers go in peace," Declan called. "Oh, I should warn ye, the reinforcements yer expecting from the woods? They won't be joining ye." A chuckle echoed through the air. "They're . . . all tied up at the moment."

"We have hostages upstairs," the man hollered. "Don't make us execute one."

"No, you really don't, General Sackett," Miles hollered, his voice sounding far stronger than he appeared. "Don't make us execute your men because you're a sadistic asshole."

"Corporal Philson." The man — General Sackett — suddenly sounded gleeful. "It's so good to hear your voice, son. Come downstairs." His voice darkened. "That's an order."

You okay, beloved? Nereo stared at his cat, worried about how he would react to that.

Warren scoffed in Nereo's mind. *I told you, I don't feel that compulsion anymore.*

Glad to hear it.

Nereo peered at Miles, wondering how he was fairing. The big blond's face was red, and the way he scowled accentuated the scar creasing his left brow. He curled his lip into a sneer as he pinned an angry gaze toward the stairway.

"I ain't your son, Sackett," Miles bellowed. "You're not even my stepfather anymore."

The scent of Miles's hatred and rage for the man downstairs filled the hallway.

"And if I find out that you found us because you put another tracking chip on me, I swear to god, I'm going to beat your ass, general or not."

General Sackett had the audacity to laugh. "You stupid morons. You're nothing but lab rats." The sneer in Sackett's voice could be heard loud and clear. "That's all you were ever good for, boy, to be experimented on. Sorry excuse for a soldier. I put tracking chips in all my projects." A growl entered General Sackett's voice as he bellowed, "I order you all to get your asses down here!"

The sound of doors opening caught Nereo's attention. He spotted Crew and David exiting their rooms. They headed toward them, and he offered them both a reassuring smile.

When they didn't respond, Nereo took a closer look at them. Their eyes seemed a little glazed, and their expressions remained flat. As Crew came abreast of Miles, he reached for his team member, attempting to wrench the gun from his grip.

"Shit," Nereo muttered. "They're still under his thumb." *Keep him down.* He sent the silent order to Warren, who snarled in response.

Although Miles wouldn't be willing to shoot his friends, he still fought, using the gun butt as a weapon. Unfortunately, having just gotten out of a coma, his strength quickly waned. Crew and David wrested the gun from Miles's hold, then slammed the butt into his forehead, causing him to slump to the floor.

Nereo grabbed the weapon's barrel, ignoring the burn from the metal of the discharged firearm. With a squeeze and twist, he bent the barrel, rendering it inoperable. That didn't mean it wouldn't give him quite the headache if Crew managed to hit him with it.

Slamming his fist into David's face, Nereo pulled his punch at the last second. Blood sprayed across the walls as the altered's head snapped back. He stumbled a few steps before catching himself.

That gave Nereo the opportunity he needed to slice through the gun's strap, allowing him to pull it free of Crew's body. Having been inside the man's head many times, he knew his vulnerabilities. Crew had a weak tendon in his calf from injuries, and he delivered a swift kick to it. With a cry, the man went down.

With blood pouring down his face, David grabbed wildly for him. Nereo let him get close, only to grip one arm and spin him, reeling him in so David's back was to his chest. Swiftly getting him in a headlock, Nereo carefully cut off the man's air supply.

Eyeing Crew, Nereo watched as he tried to regroup. He was using the wall to climb back to his feet, obviously still intent on doing Sackett's bidding. Before Crew could manage it, David went limp in Nereo's hold. He counted to five before carefully lowering him to the floor and checking his pulse.

Alive.

Then Nereo swept out his foot and sent Crew sprawling back to the floor.

"That's enough."

Nereo spun around, and his blood ran cold. A man held a gun to Warren's head, using the barrel to nudge him off the sprawled soldier. While his beloved growled softly, he obeyed, letting the other man up.

Evidently, his amazing beloved had been too busy watching him and forgot to keep his eye on the stairs.

I'm so sorry.

Don't apologize. Nereo did his best to send a sense of calm to his beloved. *We're not beaten, yet.*

"Now, then." Sackett had mouse-brown hair and a mustache trying to hide a weak chin. "What kind of shifter are you, I wonder?"

Arching one brow, Nereo shook his head. "Not a shifter."

Sackett's eyes narrowed, and he sneered. "I watched you fight. You have their strength and speed. You can't lie to me." Puffing up his chest, as if that would make him more intimidating. "Tell me what kind of shifter you are."

"He's a—"

Nereo didn't allow Crew to finish. He whipped out a hand and smacked him in the temple. The man's eyes rolled to the back of his head, and Nereo caught him before he could hit the ground. Crew was unconscious, and Nereo bet he would wake with one hell of a headache, but he *would* wake up.

"Not a shifter," Nereo repeated, smirking.

"Tell me, or I'll shoot your kitty friend," Sackett demanded. "Now that he's shifted, he's of no use to me."

"You shoot him, and I'll cut out your heart," Nereo vowed, his eyes narrowing.

For an instant, Nereo had the satisfaction of spotting fear flash in the man's eyes. Then he cleared his throat and sniffed, as if Nereo's threats meant nothing.

"I—"

The report of a high-powered rifle rent the air. Glass from the window at the end of the hall shattered, and Sackett screamed, dropping his gun. He clutched his arm to his chest, and Nereo could not only see but smell that it was bleeding profusely. The soldier Sackett had saved dove for cover even as the general started screaming into his comms about finding the shooter and taking him out.

Except, there didn't seem to be anyone available to answer him.

Snarling, Warren lunged, pouncing on Sackett.

Sprinting down the hall with vampire speed, growing his claws and dispatching the last soldier as he moved, Nereo reached Sackett and Warren just as his lover prepared to strike.

"Beloved, don't."

Warren paused, growling. *Why the fuck not?*

As much as Nereo hated to admit it, he reminded him, "We need him alive."

CHAPTER TWELVE

I want to rip his throat out so badly right now.
Nereo rested his hand on Warren's furry shoulder, rubbing lightly. "I know, beloved." His vampire held Warren's gaze. "But he has information we need." Grimacing, Nereo added, "I was going to say you could kill him after he's sung like a canary, but I think the CIA want him."

Warren chuffed in irritation even as he backed away from Sackett. He would never consider this sack of shit as a general again. The man didn't know the meaning of honor and had no business trying to lead men.

Even bleeding and beginning to pale, Sackett sneered. "I'll never talk," he declared. "You'll never get anything out of me. I'd rather die."

Lowering to one knee beside Sackett, Nereo rested his forearm on his thigh as he leaned toward the man.

If Warren didn't miss his guess, he would say that Sackett appeared more than just a little bit nervous.

"When I told you I wasn't a shifter, I wasn't lying," Nereo commented mildly. Grinning, showing off his fangs, he asked, "Haven't you ever met a vampire before?"

"Wha?" Sackett gasped as he shook his head. "N-No. Vampires aren't real."

Smirking, Nereo waved a negligent hand at Warren. "You know that shifters are real. Why don't you believe in us?"

"I, uh—" He shook his head again. "No. Vampires aren't real."

"Sure we are," Nereo countered. His eyes hazed, his irises

bleeding to red. "Just because you don't believe in us doesn't mean we aren't real." Growing his three-inch talons, he rested one hand on Sackett's chest and reached the other toward the man's temple. "Now, I'm not even going to ask you any questions." Nereo's tone filled with an icy joy that Warren was so thankful would never be turned on him as his vampire touched the side of Sackett's face. "I'm going to delve deep into your miserable excuse for a brain and rip every secret from within its depths. I may decide to leave you drooling like a babe for the rest of your life."

That would be way too good for him. Warren project the thought into his lover before he could think better of it.

Nereo turned his head and smirked at him. "You're right, beloved. That would be way too good for him." Grinning widely at Sackett, Nereo amended, "Never mind. I'll leave your mind intact . . . mostly. That way, you can live a long life with the knowledge that we beat you."

Warren watched as Sackett's eyes glazed over a bit. The man's jaw sagged open. A squeal of pain filled the air, followed by the distinctive scent of urine.

Reeling back a couple of steps, Warren snorted. *Disgusting. He really is.*

Warren heard Nereo's mental agreement.

"Good grief." Vince's voice sounded up the stairs before they saw him. "What the hell happened up here?" Lifting his hand to his nose and mouth, Vince eyed Sackett with disgust. "What did you do, Nereo?"

Shrugging unabashedly, Nereo claimed, "Nothing the man didn't deserve."

When Nereo returned his focus to Sackett, the man flinched and whimpered.

"Gods, it's going to take forever to get the smell out of the hallway," Declan grumbled as he joined them on the landing.

Lifting his attention back to their friends, Nereo scowled at the alpha wolf. "Just what the fuck happened? How the hell did everyone but us end up outside?"

"That was my fault," Clayton peeked around the corner, wrinkling his nose. "I was setting perimeter bombs when I got snagged." His cheeks took on a deep pink hue. "Bailey came after me, and everyone else came after him. It left the house wide open." Clayton's big blue eyes were filled with remorse. "Can you ever forgive me?"

Reaching out to Nereo, Warren gave his answer. *I forgive you. I finally shifted for the first time. Cool, right? And we got the bad guy.* Then Warren offered a cat grin as he peered down the hallway at his friends and team members. *But you'll probably have some groveling to do to the others.*

Chuckling, Nereo relayed the message.

Clayton stared at everyone with huge eyes. "Yeah. Yeah, totally." His eyes lit up. "I'll make some special bombs for them. They'll love 'em."

"Is anyone hurt?" Lark squeezed around the corner. His gaze skipped right over Sackett to the mess beyond. "Oh, my god. Is that Miles?" With a graceful leap, Lark jumped the downed human and hustled to Miles. "What's he doing out here?"

"He woke up," Nereo answered. "The gunfire yanked him out of his coma." He turned to Vince. "I dredged this asshole's mind, but if you want to do it again"—he grinned evilly at Sackett—"two eyes are always better than one."

"On it."

With those simple words, Vince apparently took over the responsibility of Sackett, for Nereo rose and beckoned to Warren. "You ready to shift back, beloved?" He guided him back into their room. "I'd really like to check you over to make certain you're not hurt."

Even as Warren reminded him of something important— *You're the one who was in a fight, not me*—he tried to think of how to shift. *Um, how do I change back?*

Nereo stuck his head out the door. "Hey, Vince, can

Frankie give us a hand for a sec?"

Declan answered. "He's in Sackett's mind, at the moment. What do ye need?"

"Warren needs a hand shifting back to human form," Nereo replied.

"Ah, of course. Here I come," the alpha wolf replied, appearing a few seconds later, striding into the bedroom. "Okay, here's what ye do."

After five minutes of deep breathing and mentally concentrating on forming fingers and toes, all Warren actually had to do was think about Nereo. He wanted to be kissed by him, held by him, fucked by him. His cat immediately released its hold on their form, and Warren once more turned human.

Warren received plenty of praise from Declan, and Warren didn't tell the alpha that his advice only sort of helped. The male had assisted him in many other ways, after all. He wasn't about to alienate him just because of one little mistake.

"Here's some sweats, beloved," Nereo pressed the fabric into his hands.

Declan chuckled and turned away, saying, "Ye'll get used to a certain degree of nudity, Nereo."

"I suppose." His vampire really didn't sound too sure.

"Oh, my god," Lark hollered. "What the hell happened to Crew and David?" Dismay colored his voice.

With his sweats around his hips, Warren hurried from the room. "That was that asshole Sackett's fault," he declared, scowling in the direction the man had been, but he'd been taken away at some point while he was in the bedroom shifting. "They're still too far under his compulsion, so when he started bellowing orders, they tried to obey." Sighing, Warren took Nereo's hand. "They're the ones that knocked Miles back out. Nereo stopped them from going to Sackett and taking Miles, too, and I know he was as gentle as possible, but when you're in that mindset . . . you just keep trying until you're unconscious, so that's what he had to do."

Lark sighed, sadness filling his eyes. "We'll get them patched up." Glancing between everyone, he ordered, "Please carry them back to their rooms." He pinned a frown on Nereo. "Please tell me exactly where you hit them, so I can get them as comfortable as swiftly as possible."

Nereo nodded. "They're good men," he said sadly. "I hated doing it."

They spent the next half an hour following Lark's instructions. Crew's leg was bandaged and ointment slathered over his temple, which was already turning a spectacular shade of black and blue. David's nose was cleaned and set so it would heal straight. Cream was wiped on the slight mottling around his throat, as well.

All in all, Lark admitted they didn't come out too worse for wear, considering they were pitted against a vampire enforcer.

Enforcer Kade poked his head in just as they were wrapping up. "Hey, Alpha." His smile appeared sheepish. "Agent Craigson and his boss are downstairs. Guess they came to take custody of Sackett personally. They want to talk to you." Lowering his voice, the big enforcer whispered, "I don't think his boss is too happy right now, considering the shape Sackett's in."

"Frankly, I don't give a damn," Declan grumbled. His deep gray eyes narrowed. "Why don't ye send him up, so they can see the mess they made?"

Kade grinned broadly. "Yes, Alpha." Then he hurried from the room.

"He's where?" a man asked a moment later. "Holy shit. What happened here?"

"Oh, the usual," Kade replied gruffly. "Assholes trying to

kidnap and experiment on people."

"Speaking of kidnapping," Nereo piped up. "These guys may have tracking devices inserted somewhere on their bodies."

"Good grief," Lark grumbled, shaking his head. "How could I have forgotten to check for that before now?" Crossing to a bureau, he opened a door, then a drawer within, and pulled out a fancy-looking electronic device. "Let's see what we can find."

Lark growled softly. "Of course. Deep in the hip like Sekani's was." Shaking his head, he muttered, "At least these guys are already out, so they won't feel it too much."

"What the hell is he doing to those men?"

Warren turned to find a wiry, black man standing in the doorway. With fire filling his brown eyes, he strode toward Lark, but Declan intercepted him. Crossing his arms over his chest, the man repeated his question. "Why is he cutting them open?"

Declan indicated the two men laid out in the room. "These are two of the soldiers who were altered against their will," he explained softly. "They can still be compelled by a dominant personality if Bailey isn't around to counter the order." Grimacing, Declan stated, "We just learned that there's tracking chips in them, which is how Sackett tracked us to this area. Lark is removing them so no one else can do the same."

The stranger's jaw clenched and released, but he finally jerked a nod and stuck out his hand. "I'm Agent Reiste. I've heard good things about you from Agent Craigson. Thanks for catching Sackett and having your vampire friends do a mind-sweep on him. The information they've turned up will be invaluable in taking out their entire organization."

"Ye're very welcome," Declan replied with a tight smile. "I certainly hope they're removed quietly. They threaten the safety and anonymity of all paranormals, and I know neither of us want that."

Agent Reiste's gaze once again settled on the sleeping men as he murmured, "No. No, we certainly don't."

"Okay, Warren." Lark beckoned to him. "You're next."

With a grimace, Warren headed over to the doctor to be scanned and have the chip removed, because of course, Lark found one.

Nereo wrapped his arms around Warren's torso and urged him to lean against him. As Lark worked on his hip, his vampire lover licked and nipped up and down his neck, doing a hell of a job of distracting him. Feeling his man's lips on his sensitive claiming scar, Warren had to do deep breathing exercises to keep his cock in check, even with the pain caused by being cut open—local anesthetic or not.

Seeing his predicament just made Nereo chuckle and begin whispering all the things he wanted to do to and with Warren once they could retreat to their bedroom.

Warren felt his breathing speed up, and he couldn't wait to experience everything Nereo promised him. After all, Sackett was going to get his just desserts, the CIA was involved in the clearing out of the man's organization, and his vampire was planning to stay in Stone Ridge until the dust settled. Evidently, Nereo had quite a bit of vacation time stored up.

In Warren's opinion, with his vampire by his side, life was finally starting to look damn near perfect . . . and he couldn't wait to get started living it.

About the Author

Charlie started writing fantasy when she was eight, and after stumbling onto her first erotic romance at age nineteen, she realized her true calling. She now focuses on writing gay erotic romance, normally of the paranormal variety, with heroes of all kinds. With the help and support of her husband, Charlie finally fulfilled one of her life-long goals . . . move to acreage with her horses. You can often find her curled up with her laptop and a cup of tea or glass of wine, creating her next adventure. Charlie enjoys exploring the mountains of her new Oregon home on horseback, 4-wheeler, or motorcycle.

She can be reached at ch.richards2010@yahoo.com

Or visit her at www.charlie-richards.com.